Falling Up

in

The City of Angels

By Connor Judson Garrett

Dedication

To my mom, Echo and dad, Kevin,

Thank you for the emotional and moral support.

A novel is a long journey — one I wouldn't

have gotten to the end of without you.

Table of Contents

Chapter One: New Age Alchemy

I had just graduated college when my Granddaddy Bob died. He was a music man, and Buddy Holly's best friend. He'd left Lubbock, Texas behind for Nashville. I think maybe his spirit played some part in me leaving the only place I'd ever lived to go west. He would always call me Tony in his Texas Hill Country drawl, and he was the first person to make me sit still long enough to watch the sunset.

I loved my girlfriend Isabella, but wasn't sure we could make things work. I wasn't really sure about anything in my life, including me. I knew I wanted to be a writer and was working on a novel. My parents warned me against moving to L.A. I barely had any money or a plan. But I'd seen *The Doors* and had fallen in love with the Venice Canals . . . that grungy, wannabe-Italian, seaside town with its Mediterranean climate and hobos.

My old friend Ricky was broken up about a girl who he'd moved out there with. She was finishing up school at Loyola Marymount University, and he was working and smoking himself into oblivion. Things ended badly. He and I both have a habit of that. He's one of my tribe: the mad ones, always aching or going numb, then thawing out by the heat of a new lover or muse. He offered me a place to stay.

Growing up, Ricky had been better friends with my older brother Aiden than me. But somewhere along the way, they had a falling out, and we had a falling in. We went to raves together. My first time being drunk was with him. All it took was nine or ten Hard Lemonades. The number doesn't matter much . . . there's just no way to make that sound cool. When he wanted to, Ricky had a devilish charisma, the sort that invites your own demons to come out and play, to run amok in the night. But his heart was good and pure enough.

I wanted Isabella to come with me, but she broke up with me certain that I hadn't even mentioned moving away. But I had invited her. Truth is, I'd been a lousy boyfriend up to that point, a real scoundrel, yet in my twisted way, I loved her. We'd traded hearts and eyes and words, and all the things hidden in the shadows beneath our flesh where the love lived in our bones.

I packed up as many clothes as I could fit into one bag and a suitcase, and a speaker to play music on and had about $1,800 to my name. I flew out with all my visions, my soul stirring, and a steadily growing certainty that I was heading where I needed to go. I couldn't say how long I'd be gone and it was irrelevant. All that mattered was then, and right then and there, I needed to go somewhere to draw a line over *what if*. I wanted to be somebody, a writer, and many other things.

Ricky picked me up from Los Angeles International Airport. We drove down the hill overlooking the westside. We passed Loyola Marymount University. The cool, just right air blew in through the windows and the streets were empty that time of night and we talked the whole ride about how wild and grand life would be.

We got a one-bedroom place right by the beach. He paid the bulk of the rent, while I pitched in $500 a month. It was a light blue apartment on South Venice Boulevard. I slept on the couch, so the living room was essentially my bedroom. It was a cramped place, but when you're living in Bohemian paradise, you shouldn't be inside other than to sleep. We were a couple hundred yards from the beach and the basketball courts and the skate park. The smell of weed was perpetually wafting in through the windows we kept cracked, mingling with the incense Ricky would burn. A nightclub, James Beach, where all the college kids flocked to, backed up to our garage. A mural of great people like Einstein and Tesla was painted just a few buildings closer to the boardwalk up the street. And a mural of Jim Morrison, the Poet

3

of Dogtown, was on another building just a street or two over. Inspiration was everywhere if your eyes were simply open.

I didn't have a job or any concrete plans other than knowing I would write and live and burn for it under the California sun. I started helping Ricky make calls and send emails for QuickRecruiter during the morning hours. We were link-building or trying to get one website's URL linked onto another website. The goal was to drive web traffic from one source to another and to raise your search rank in Google's algorithm. It was dreadfully boring, but we made the most of it. We were telemarketers without selling any sort of product. Our only hurdle was indifference. But the pay was decent enough and we had time freedom, if not financial freedom.

Most days we were done by one or two in the afternoon. I'd bring my leather pad to the beach and lay under the sun writing the day away, working on poetry and a novel that wasn't going anywhere. That was my feeling at least — that all the things I wanted to move weren't and all the things I wished to stay were slipping. I'd check out the pretty girls on the beach, but watching was enough. Just that they were there. I didn't want any of them, but they were good for my spirits for a while. That's how it is with pretty girls. They get a man's blood flowing away from his brain, which makes him think a little less and live a little more. This is why rich men surround themselves with pretty women — because they can, of course. But also, to be intoxicated by beauty just long enough to convince themselves the world's one great, big lucid dream.

The first girl I had a real conversation with in L.A. was a blonde, curly-headed New Jerseyan whose voice was hoarse. I was walking on the beach as the sun was setting when I saw Jessie — that was her name — dancing and smiling and laughing as if she had heard the funniest joke. She was being photographed in her swimsuit beneath the Venice Pier. As I walked past, she waved me over. "Hey," she said, "can you pretend to be my boyfriend?" We fell into place with each other naturally. It went well enough that we agreed to meet up later that night. That was another thing I learned about people in L.A. — if they say you'll meet at 7, expect them to be there at 7:30 or 8 and don't be the least bit surprised. Just go with it. Time is different out there. Nobody is counting the hours and the minutes. On the west coast, everything is measured in flow and vibrations, and everyone does what they want to do and nothing else.

We met at Hinano's, a dive bar on Washington Street right by the pier. The locals and the regular fixtures of Venice Beach hung around there playing pool, drinking beer, and eating the free popcorn. Heavily tattooed bikers with Vatos insignia hunkered around one table. Jessie knew everybody by name and had this way of making all of their faces light up. We drank cheap beers. She told me she was planning on moving to Spain. She needed to get out of this town. I wondered why anyone would ever want to leave. I hardly knew her, but it made me a little sad. I hadn't yet developed the ability to just let the world keep turning. If there's something I've learned, it's not to twist Fate by the arm.

Jessie was confident. Not like the coy college girls or the broken cougars I'd mixed souls with. She didn't share details of her life to impress or to woo. She was unapologetically herself, which was admirable in a city of illusions. After a couple of beers and a hotdog, we left for some funk club to meet her French girlfriend. I'm awful with names, but never forget a face. It was something like Chloe or Camille and she was content dancing the night away in her friend's shadow. Twice a week they went to ballroom dance together. Their grace was juxtaposed by my Jagger-esque moves. For a brief moment, Jessie and

I danced together, but you can feel chemistry or a lack of. That spontaneous, reaction between two people. And ours fizzled out right then and there. We danced together a little more. Then the band played *Sara Smile* and Jessie and the French girl belted out every lyric and spun each other all around the room, dancing like dervishes. A voluptuous Latin woman in a red skintight dress with pretty lips grabbed me by the hand and led me to the middle of the dancefloor. I'd noticed her when we first came in. She was with a man, who could have easily been three or four hundred pounds. He had a video camera and recorded her wherever she moved. "Who is that?" I asked. "He's just a friend," she said. In a way she was telling the truth. He wasn't her boyfriend or her husband. But he was more than just a friend.

Somehow or another, Jessie and I wound up dancing together again. The Latin woman joined us. She grabbed ahold of Jessie and caressed her as they moved, while I sort of awkwardly danced around them. The Latin woman's pimp or client or whatever the hell he was kept recording. Somewhere, besides in our own memories, that night has been rewound and replayed. And then the evening was over as suddenly as if someone pressed stop. We went our separate ways. Her, with thoughts of Spain. Me, buzzing with excitement for all of the possibilities a new beginning inspires.

Ricky and I kept making our calls and sending emails every morning. We tried on different voices and tactics to keep it interesting. He'd lay a terrible southern drawl on thick. Occasionally, I'd throw in a cockney British accent. We had a quota for the amount of calls and emails we sent, but the only thing that really mattered were the results. Ricky had a silver tongue, but I had to stick to the script. He was encouraging, always telling me how bad he was when he first started doing it. "People can sense your energy, man," he'd say. "It's not about the words. It's how you say them."

We finished our day's work and walked a couple hundred feet from our apartment to the basketball courts. A crackhead was having an imaginary argument off to the side, but the breeze was blowing in, the sun was beating down, and everything was alright. We shot for a while. A guy in his fifties who looked like he could've been an actor once upon a time, came over to shoot with us. Rob was his name. We'd run into him over and over again and he'd ask us our names every time and we'd tell him facts about himself as we learned new details about his life. And he'd look at us like mystics. Rob had done acid a few too

8

many times, or had the wrong kind if there's a right kind, and his memory had turned to shit. But he seemed destined to be a recurring character in our story and Ricky and I liked him even if he couldn't remember who we were.

The graffitied palm trees swayed back and forth and cool beads of sweat rolled down our backs and there was life and energy and movement. We were living the dream simply because we believed in it. But in a short time, Ricky wanted to go back to the apartment and recede into his cocoon. That's when I realized my dear friend was hurting badly. At the time, I couldn't fathom being miserable in the City of Angels. The fun-loving, mischievous savage I grew up with was a shell of himself. He was in there still somewhere. But my visions of us roaming Dog Town like two fiends howling at the moon would have to wait. We shared an unspoken agreement — I was an ear and a pal, and he would help me navigate the Promised Land and learn how to climb the corporate ladder. He'd be a shaman for me.

I got used to going out alone. I carried my black notebook and pen with me down to Hinano's, which was a short walk away from our apartment. When you write, it changes how you see the world. You become an active observer. You learn people's secrets and histories before they tell them. You see patterns and develop intuition. That's how it is. I'd hear the different tones of drunken laughter passing through the alleys and could decipher them. Some were joyful, some were desperate.

When I got to the bar, I sat down in a seat near the pool tables. I'd play every now and then — that was half the reason I came, but I liked to watch the characters revolve in and out of the dive bar. Most were regulars. Los Angeles is a metropolis of transplants — everyone comes with a dream from Chicago or someplace you've never heard of that can only be described by its proximity to another place. The locals can read faces. They can spot the transplants. They've seen it a thousand times before — people passing through what was once their beloved ghetto by the sea, bright-eyed and hopeful, comparing reality to the dream.

I gave myself away as new, or naive. Whoever it was throwing herself around the room, desperate to be caught or seen always ended up in the chair next to me. They'd ask what I was writing or doing, then grow bored and stumble off drunk or high into the night. As the nights went on, I'd go from one bar to another, and see what was going on. Jim Morrison's old haunt Hinano's, the Venice Whaler, Townhouse, a speakeasy lounge that played funk in the basement and mostly 90s hip-hop on the first floor, the Rooftop Bar at Hotel Erwin with its birdseye view. I bounced around these places and never knew what I expected to find. Sometimes I left with longing, a contagious longing, a feverish delirium that turned the shadows into old lovers. Everybody wants to be seen. Hungry eyes, and tequila-soaked minds romanced the dark.

I stepped away from Dogtown and onto the pier, surrounded by the ocean and a few old men and Chicanos fishing off the sides late into the night. Pigeons and seagulls cooed, pecking at crumbs and cigarette butts. I traced the rooftops with my eyes through the sultry sky with its scattered, light-polluted stars, all the way to the mountains just past the Santa Monica Ferris Wheel.

This is L.A. I thought, I'm really here.

I have a habit of falling in love with everything: colors, light, shadows, a breeze, the lines of a building, a fragrance drifting off a flower or a girl — and then, all I want to do is remember it forever exactly as it was and give it to everyone so they can feel it or see it and hold onto it for safekeeping. A rollerblader dressed in American flag swim trunks and a star-spangled banner tank top zipped in a circle around the end of the pier with a boombox on his shoulder, blasting *American Woman*. And he was gone again, darting back toward the shore. We could all be seen in one of two ways: as caricatures of ourselves, playing bit parts in the bigger picture of LaLa Land, or as people loving something so hard that our obsessions consumed us. In the scheme of things, his vision of himself as a real patriot was no more ridiculous than my insistence on being a serious writer. He was after the same and only noble and honest pursuit.

I met each day in my new home with verve. I was looking for signs, eager to hear the words of the curbside prophets. I believed in magic. I believed that lightning could strike, that the stars would align, and Fate would take it easy on me. But the fact remained, I was still jobless and bumming off the grace of my friend. After we were done making our calls for the day, I strolled along the boardwalk, asking every shop and store if they were hiring. They weren't, but I wasn't ready to pull a Van Gogh and slice off my ear to join the Venice Beach Freakshow just yet.

"How was the job search?" Ricky would ask. "We'll see," I'd reply. The catch-22 nowadays is that most entry-level jobs require years of experience. It all seemed a bit oxy-moronic. I was a little envious of my friend's ability to glide through life with ease. But his mind was designed for the digital age. He told me once that he felt like he could speak to computers. It wasn't farfetched.

At night, Ricky and I went around longboarding from one restaurant or bar to another. I could barely ride, but when in California, you have to cruise. I handed my resume out to the managers and whoever would take the time to speak with me. College kids on their way to Canal Club and James Beach flowed like water around the homeless in their tents and makeshift beds. That's how it goes in the Land of the Free; opulence and squalor are step-siblings with little in common but a shared address. If you work hard enough, if you're smart enough, if you're strong enough, you can have what you want in the Land of Opportunity — that's the narrative, at least. We're taught to believe in the prosperity gospel. We equate wealth with merit and poverty with defective character. It's bullshit. Sure, some people don't want to work, some are downright lazy, but plenty of people work themselves to the bone and have nothing to show for by the time they're all but ready to turn to dust.

As we rode back to the apartment, passing the rows of tents, I didn't see laziness or the tired narrative people use to numb their compassion — "They must have a drug problem, they're gonna spend any money they get ahold of booze." I saw myself. I saw Ricky. I thought about how lucky we were to have grown up middle class with enough advantages to take a few risks and be alright regardless of the outcome. I didn't see weakness. I saw men and women who simply had no one to catch them when they fell.

As I drifted to sleep on the couch that night, I listened to someone digging through our trash, glass bottles clinking against each other, papers crinkling. And I thought about how hard life can be, hard enough to break the spirit and how heaven and hell exist here on earth, stacked on top of one another.

A couple nights later, Ricky decided he wanted to venture out of the apartment. We went to Club Zanzibar over in Santa Monica. We strolled in a little buzzed to save on drinks. The place was dim-lit with a lounge vibe and the DJ played 90s and early 2000s hip-hop and R&B; everything from Ginuwine and Blackstreet to Tupac and Biggie. Everybody was dancing and after a few Jack and Cokes, Ricky and I started scoping out the dancefloor. I'm sure we weren't as discreet as we thought. "Woah," we'd say to each other. "She's alright." And we'd split up in our separate pursuits. We floated around, dancing and mingling.

There was no scorekeeping, no counts or objectives other than to be uncomfortable enough to learn something new about ourselves and the other people in the room. If we ever had a goal, it was simply to drown our insecurities by being stranded in the types of situations where you can't afford to have any.

A go-go dancer moved like a flame on stage. I watched her spellbound out of the corner of my eye. She was petite with red hair and reminded me of a girl I knew, who was involved in some of the most exciting and disastrous moments of my college days. Her eyes flickered. She caught me staring and moved to the side of the stage near me and held her gaze steady. Ricky came back over and we leaned against the stage, drinking whiskey and talking in the dark about the things we admired.

After a while, we stepped outside into the night for a change of scene. A man with cornrows and a backpack, who smelled like urine approached a group of sorority girls. "Any of you got a cigarette?" he said. They all looked at each other, communicating nervously with their eyes. Each waited on one or the other to answer, hoping their go-away silence would do the trick. "Your husbands are gonna beat you," he erupted. The bouncer stood idly by the door, listening to the man's threats. I got between the man and the girls. I hate fighting and am not any sort of tough guy, but I was afraid he was going to try to hurt them. He staggered in a circle around me, glaring with contempt.

Then he backed away. The red-headed go-go dancer with the pixie haircut had come outside to smoke a cigarette. She stood by herself near the curb, looking up at the sky. The man went over to her. "Can I bum one off ya?" he said.

"No, only got a couple left," she said.

"You're a stuck up bitch," he said. He raised his hand as if he was going to throw a punch at her. I went over and pushed him back a couple of feet to create distance. "Fuck you," he shouted.

When I'm livid like I was, I can hardly speak at all, but for some reason, what I was thinking came out perfectly clear. "You're a misogynistic fuck," I said. He had the blankest of all the blank expressions in the world, which gave away the fact that he had no clue what misogynistic means.

When Ricky saw his hesitation, he burst out laughing. At this point, the man felt the need to prove himself, so he took off his backpack and unzipped it to show me a piece of paper. "I'm taking

classes," he said, "I know what that word means." Ricky started laughing

even harder. Finally, after all that the bouncer spoke up and told us if

we were going to fight to do it in the parking lot across the street. The

man started to walk across the street. I broke into a jog towards the

parking lot and started waving him to hurry up as if I was eager and had

been waiting for that moment for all of my life.

He stopped dead in his tracks. "Come on," I said. He began

telling me he didn't have time to fight, and he walked away cursing

and muttering to himself. We got ready to leave. The pixie dancer

said *thank you* and I got to be the good guy for once.

Ricky and I talked about that a lot — what it means to be good

or bad. We both agreed we occupied this gray space in between. If

Judgment Day were to come, we'd be stuck in limbo, not holy enough

for the angels, but not quite wicked enough for the demons. Aree Ogir,

another good friend of mine, talked about that as well — what's right

and wrong, the meaning of life, the purpose of humanity; all the big

things that religions assume ownership of. But Aree was spiritual; not

in the cliché, Santa Monica yogi, tripping on ayahuasca, who'd found

chemical enlightenment type of way. He learned Hebrew and read the

Torah, he'd studied the Bible, read the Quran and listened to thinkers new and old. That's all to say, he was a man of substance.

Aree told me once that relativism, the moral framework I suppose Ricky and I were working off of, is eating away at the soul of mankind, and that there's a disregard for the chain of authenticity. He'd say, "The mystical is largely absent and postmodernism has sentenced the sacred to death. We can't even face the sacred in ourselves, let alone in others or even mundane things. Mankind is consumed from the outside by materialism in the real and abstract, and science should be a part of the sacred, but it has been reduced to dogma; it's become monolithic. The mystic should test his own claims. Madness is a pack of wolves and all the apex predators holding them at bay have been bound by the zeitgeist. There are many things in the modern age being touted as sacred, which are not, and if you approach them, you will be martyred; capitalism, statism, individual morality. Relativism and fundamentalism are both false idols. Humans are prone to all sorts of madness."

He'd go on like this, cryptically darting from point to point, each of which he could expound upon infinitely, but everything was connected. "I've been drawn towards traditionalism to hold the wolves

18

at bay. Kali yuga, man. Look it up, we're in it," he told me. "I feel alienated by the spirit of the modern world. I'm burdened for my children. Don't get me wrong. We don't need to be pioneers or deny the certain reality of what's around us. But the alchemists of old dealt with the same problem; the conversion of the base element into something pure."

Ricky and I were new age alchemists. He'd headed west to get away from his mother. Nothing is crazy when you've grown up with it. On the opposite side of the country, he'd learned to catch himself getting wild-eyed and overly theoretical. I was searching for purpose, the elixir of life that transmutes the soul into something divine. We'd both practiced our mysticism with love, but every romantic encounter had turned from a base element to shit instead of gold.

The quest itself wasn't new. My whole life I'd been keenly aware of mortality, the simple fact that every one of us will die. I would credit that to funeral-hopping as a kid. But because of it, each day has always felt desperately important for as long as I can remember. The only people I could understand were the ones burning for life, burning to understand the secret, the ones who weren't afraid to accept the truth no matter how glorious or grim it may be.

Ricky and I went to kick the soccer ball over at a field in Playa Vista. We passed one of YouTube's offices along the way. YouTube, Google, SnapChat — all the big players in tech were moving into the area, giving it the unofficial title Silicon Beach. We'd both grown up playing soccer. It was one of the few places where being different was to my advantage even before I'd learned to hide my strange a little better. For Ricky it was the same way. Our instincts, aggressiveness, and ability to improvise were perfectly suited for the game, and the field was the one place we felt like we belonged.

Ricky and I took shots on goal and practiced crosses and wound up playing three versus three. We joined with another young guy, Hector. I think he said he was a pipefitter, or something like that. But he was kind and ambitious enough and told us his plans to travel Europe in the summer. He asked all types of questions — *Where were we from? How long ago did we move out there? What did we come there for?* He was feeling us out. I didn't fault Hector for wanting to climb. Besides, he was interested in making new friends as well. We didn't have many out there, so we agreed to hang out soon.

I met up with Hector that weekend over in Venice Beach. We kicked around along the shoreline, dribbling the ball around the tide, making cuts as if it were a defender. We took turns attacking each other, offense against defense. Then we went and worked out on the bars near the Muscle Beach Gym that Arnold Schwarzenegger made world famous. My dad always told me the key to winning people over is to be interested in them instead of trying to be interesting to them. That's one of the things that stood out about Hector; he was interested in everything.

After an afternoon in the sun, he asked if we could smoke. I showed him our apartment just a stone's throw away. Hector ran to his car and brought back the strangest, balloon-like device. Ricky's eyes communicated frustration that I'd allowed a near-stranger into our space. He was keen about "protecting our energy" and keeping it pure. He'd burn sage when something didn't feel right to him. But when Hector offered to share his weed out of that balloon, Ricky let his suspicions go. At least until later that night when we all agreed to hit the town.

That night Hector came back to our place. He told me last minute that he was also bringing his cousin Carlos with him. They showed up at our door around ten. Carlos dressed every bit like the stereotypical cholo gangster; he wore a crisp white oversized tee, plaid short sleeve button down with just the top buttoned, baggy Dickies 874

original cut, and Chuck Taylors. He seemed decent enough, a little

sketchy, but not malicious. Ricky was still suspicious about him, so he

started talking to Carlos about anything and everything, befriending our

new cholo pal to cut off any strangeness at its head.

It didn't take long for Carlos to tell us about growing up in

Inglewood. He alluded to wickedness, saying how he used to snap if

someone looked at him wrong. He used to be this. He used to be that,

but he'd straightened up. You can tell a lot about someone based on

what they take pride in. Carlos lit up as he spoke of his machismo,

verbally pounding his chest. Hector, who was more restrained and

better at reading a room, put his arm around Carlos' shoulder and

shifted his cousin onto a softer subject. We stepped out of 31 South

Venice Boulevard into the night.

We walked along Pacific Avenue on down to the strung-up

Venice sign till we reached Townhouse, a speakeasy lounge nightclub

right on the fringe of the boardwalk. It was a magnet for the rebels and

the misfits, the new age hipsters, with their tattooed skin and marked

souls. Carlos jutted his jaw out and clenched it and held his pants up by the front of his belt as he circled girls here and there like some sort of awkward vulture.

I pretended not to be observing him. "Hey girl," he'd say. "Wanna dance?" He'd slide up behind them and they'd just as soon move away into any other part of the room. "She's fine as hell," he'd say to me. He switched tactics; he stopped asking and started just grabbing them by the waist and going straight for the kill. They'd wriggle out of Carlos' grasp. "She's not my type," he'd turn and say. "Stuck up *puta.*"

Hector had a soft spot for Carlos. At first, I didn't understand why. But when he saw his cousin floundering, he played wingman and introduced him to women around the room after opening up the initial conversation. Ricky remained a quiet observer to all of this. Carlos was constantly proving himself. He committed the cardinal sin of trying to be interesting instead of being interested. Eventually, he resorted to leaning back against the bar, commenting about how the girls all thought they were too good for him. The thing is, usually it's the other way around — we decide that for ourselves.

We did another walkthrough of the bar, roaming the dark for God knows what. We checked out the basement. The deejay played

90s bump n' grind and Carlos decided to try his luck again, getting behind any girl who wasn't coupled up or in a group of her friends. Ricky was grinning and drinking whiskey and watching the whole mad theater of life play out in the dark of the club — the desperation, the joy, the people eyeing somebody eyeing someone else. And Carlos was stumbling around between it all, crashing the show with bad acting and poor timing, but really he was the same as us. Or we were the same as him. We all just want to be peeled raw till all the ugly parts are exposed, till everything underneath it all is naked. Yet we peacock and strut and do our best to hide our confused, tender little hearts.

We stepped back out into the night. Carlos started talking about his skills as a rapper after Ricky told him about his passion for producing music. Ricky goaded him on to freestyle as the stray, midnight long boarders rolled past, wheels roaring on the asphalt. His lines trailed off into mumbles, faltering with his confidence, but Hector pushed him to keep going. I think Carlos believed Ricky was secretly auditioning him, and by the time we reached the apartment, ready to say goodnight, our cholo pal was already making plans of releasing his mixtape. After they went on their way, Ricky said, "Now we have to make sure the doors our constantly locked." He was convinced Carlos was looking for any way out of Inglewood, and would be back to rob

the place.

Chapter Two: Dogtown Delirium

The shine of my new life took on the patina of loneliness. To gain something you have to lose something. I got a call from my mom that my Uncle Mark was sick back home. Aggressive leukemia. Death was in his blood and bones. He was a great father and a great husband, and I don't mean that he just brought home money and put food on the table and was simply there. He cherished my aunt and you could feel it. She wore his love like a blanket, cozy and warm, and she knew she was safe. As a dad, he was tender to my cousins, his three boys. And he raised each of them differently — he was hardest on the oldest one so he'd be ready to lead his younger brothers; he was gentle with his middle son and just encouraged him to keep fighting; and he just held Declan, my youngest cousin tight as if he somehow knew they'd have the least time together. He coached all their sports teams and gave everyone's kids time on the field. His pants had grass stains from throwing the baseball or the football in the yard with his boys or whatever sport was in season.

My uncle saw the world in black and white, right and wrong, righteous versus wicked. He didn't buy into the relativism that my good friend Aree saw plaguing modern society. He loved his friends, he loved everybody -- honestly and purely and tenaciously.

He saved my life when I was child. I couldn't swim and fell off the dock into a lake. I was sinking fast and flailing my arms and it was getting darker and becoming more hopeless. I remember it happening in slow motion. Then he reached down and snatched me out of the water. He spent the afternoon fishing for the shoes I was wearing and miraculously managed to hook them out of that murky lake, too. That would've all been enough right there. But he cared and kept caring in all the time I knew him. He wanted our family to thrive and gave advice both solicited and unsolicited, but whatever he said was what he believed you needed to hear.

My uncle was one of my heroes, but I couldn't be like him. He was too good, too in-the-right, too blameless to emulate. But watching the way he lived his life taught me that the heart doesn't have a finite capacity for love. The more of it you give, the more it grows, the more powerful it becomes, serving as a magnet of spiritual energy.

And then he got sick. My old belief, that bleak nihilism settled back in like the loneliest side of 3AM. Not everything happens for a reason. Life just goes on and we make the best of it. Uncle Mark would ask me what my short-term plan was, what my long-term plan was, and what I'd do in between. He asked me that when I was in high school, and back then, I didn't quite get it. But it started to make sense in L.A. — life moves forwards and backwards, it changes speeds, it changes complexities, and you have to be prepared for anything: death, taxes, and the uncertain.

I was laying on the couch, listening to the breeze and the neighbor's music pulsing through the Venice night. A pretty Mexican girl drunk on tequila and desire came out of Ricky's room naked from head to toe. She grabbed a glass of water and disappeared back into his bedroom. But the shape of her body, her curves, the way she moved — in the drowsy shadows, I saw Isabella. My heart grew heavy. I could feel it sinking in my body, full of old memories, feelings, and longing. That night, the scale of the past and the future tipped towards history.

I wanted to desecrate temples, to demarcate remembrance from creation, a line painted with irreverence. Naturally, I turned to Tinder. An addict of any sort goes to their addiction to get their fix when they're triggered: an alcoholic picks up the bottle, a cokehead calls their dealer, and a fuckboy starts swiping right. Now for the record, sex addiction is real. Some people have a thing for eating wood chips. I like women. But when I moved to L.A. I'd decided to reclaim some of my innocence. I wanted to be different, but seeing the Mexican girl like that in our apartment had me all twisted up and ready to fuck my way into oblivion.

It's soulless, but effective, having infinite options in the palm of your hand. That's what things have come to — people are terrified of authenticity. It's easier to connect with a perfect stranger on an app nowadays than it is to approach someone in a bar and strike up a conversation the old fashion way. I resented modern dating, but was a part of the problem.

The first girl I met up with from Tinder was named Bianca and she had grown up around Venice. We walked on the beach making small talk. "White boys get all attached," she said. At the time, I was well-tanned from spending the days under the California sun, so I'm not sure she knew I was white, or maybe she didn't care. Either way, to her point, I think the truth is we fall on a spectrum. Some people get attached to anyone they're with, other people avoid feelings like the plague.

I was somewhere in between. The burn was usually just a burn, a simple flicker that would fizzle out. It was rare I carried a torch for anybody. And I could always tell right away if that was even possible. In fact, because I didn't care at all what happened, Bianca was drawn to my indifference and we ended up back at my place within the hour, with her telling me to choke her. Sometimes it's making love. Sometimes it's just sex. All my restraint, my return to innocence was out the window.

I was coated in kerosene and now just the slightest brush of a passing flame grew on me like wildfire. I could feel the vices and the hedonism that I'd tried to transmute into something pure driving me mercury mad. Passion became the noblest virtue once again. The seal was broken.

Across from my apartment, three men worked late into the nights and the early mornings. Their computers illuminated their faces as they stared intently into the screens. I made up a story for them. They had a tech startup and had left everything behind to go all in on their dream. One of them was a visionary, the one who got up from his chair the most, pacing the top floor. The other two were coders, thinking in binary, translating his vision into something seamless for the world to use.

Each night, a range rover with black tinted windows cruised along the streets and the alleys. During the day, a bearded man rollerbladed up and down the boardwalk, playing the electric guitar — strumming the same songs again and again. Another man kept his hair spiked into two horns like the Tasmanian Devil and he rollerbladed all day long in a red speedo that left little to the imagination. The Jamaicans scammed tourists, kindly asking them if they'd listen to their reggae and reggaeton cds. Then they'd carry on the conversation asking the tourists their names, signing the cds for them, so they'd feel obligated to buy it after initially talking it up like a gift. I supposed their con worked well enough for them to continue doing it every day. They'd congregate like flies outside of one of the dispensaries, catching people strolling by the narrow pass between the basketball courts and the shops.

The piano man sat on his chair with his head bowed and his hair draped over his eyes. He was remembering more than he was actually playing. His fingers danced to the soundtrack of his past. An old bodybuilder, who had spent his life devoted to defining his muscle groups walked around in his Speedo like a wax figurine melting under the hot California sun. His picture would appear nine months later in an obituary. He went back to Pennsylvania and wandered off and died in a ditch. Turns out he was a legend in his craft back in the day. He was friends with Schwarzenegger during the golden age of Muscle Beach and his biceps were big enough to make the Terminator jealous. But time is a ruthless thief. To me, he was just an old man in a Speedo.

These people had been around for so long that they'd become a part of Dogtown. There was something permanent about them. The rest of us were water flowing over and around them, but they were unmoved by the current. Had they become mad or had they realized something the rest of us were still searching for?

I wrote every night. My mind fed on moonglow and starlight, tequila and the darkness where imagination thrives. I used my pen to chisel away at life and sculpt meaning of it. Some nights I sought out the mild noise of Hinano's or the Venice Whaler with their revolving cast of characters.

Ricky was growing stronger again. He was smiling more and more and getting out of the apartment. His ambitions grew as well and he was ready to shed everything that held him captive. We kept on making our calls for QuickRecruiter, and I kept applying for jobs I wasn't interested in, but money, or a lack of, quickly became my chief concern.

I went to write in Cow's End, a quiet little coffee shop on Washington Boulevard just a straight shot up from the Venice Pier. It was a dreary day. It's not always sunny in L.A. Summer is known for June Gloom. There were couches upstairs and it felt like working from home. I sunk into the leather and tried to push the steadily creeping anxiety behind. When you're fearful, the demons ever-circling your soul manifest themselves in the people you meet and the thoughts you have.

As I sat there typing away I could feel a pair of eyes watching me. "Hey," said a distinctly southern voice. "Whatcha working on there?"

"A novel," I answered reluctantly.

"Mmmm," he groaned. "I like that."

He moved to a leather chair next to the couch I was sat on.

"I'm Wolf," he said. He held out his hand. Wolf had rings on every finger.

"Is that your real name?"

"It's my spirit animal," he replied. "You're not from round here are you? You look so..." He paused as he searched for the word. "So new."

"No, I'm from Georgia."

"Ah, I'm from Birmingham, Alabama," he said.

"I have family over there," I replied. "Mountain Brook area."

"Why'd you come here?"

"The sunshine, the beach, the girls, and to try something different, I guess."

"Hmmm," he groaned. "You're running from something. Someone, really."

"No, nothing like that."

"No, you are," he said. "I can feel these things. It's energy. I was running from my family thirty years ago when I left for good. We've all got our demons, sweet boy."

I tried to resume working, but his eyes were trained on me, and I felt it was somehow rude to abruptly leave Cow's End.

"So what do you do, Wolf?"

"I'm a webcam model," he said. "People pay to watch me strip online. Lot of money in it."

"Oh, that's cool," I said. "Gotta make a living."

"They'll pay for your underwear. They'll send you things. You get fans," he said. "They'd love you."

"That's pretty wild."

I tried to feign just enough interest to be polite to my eccentric new acquaintance, while angling to head on. Then a pretty woman with pink hair in a black and white polka dot dress blew by the door frame to the upstairs backroom of the cafe. Wolf saw me watching.

"She's always around," he said. "Saw her at a party the other night. She's always with a different guy. That's part of her profession."

"Her profession?"

"She's an escort. A certified industry chick," he said. "You wanna meet her?"

"Right now?"

"Now or later," he said. "I can introduce you to lots of girls like that. People run in the same circles here. You'll cross paths over and over again."

I'm far from religious and I'm not anymore certain about the Devil than God. But some scriptures flash through my mind every so often. That was one of those times. *Be sober-minded; be watchful. Your adversary the devil prowls around like a roaring lion, seeking someone to devour.* Call them devils or whatever you'd like, but the world has its fair share of opportunists, is all. They'll listen to you. They'll watch your eyes and try to interpret your desires as written in fine print of your irises.

"I think I'm alright," I said.

He paused, searching for a new angle.

"I make jewelry," he said, holding out his ringed-hand, twirling his fingers in the light. "I give it away to people I like. I could take care of you. Make your life easier."

"I gotta get to work, Wolf."

And I left without really saying too much more. All Ricky's talk of energy and vibrations had started to rub off on me. Wolf had all the wrong energy. Cholo Carlos, by contrast, simply wanted to be loved and accepted. My new acquaintance was searching for prey instead.

That was the same week I met Jane. We matched on Tinder and managed to wade through all the small talk just long enough to go on a date. That's the other strange thing about dating apps — you end up waiting somewhere for someone you only recognize by picture, assuming they do in fact look like their picture.

It was a sunny day and a steady stream of people flowed along the sidewalks of Washington Boulevard. I remember searching the crowds for a pretty blonde talking on her phone. Then I spotted her. Jane didn't exactly stand out from the other girls. She wore a blue or turquoise dress. Or maybe that was just the color of her eyes, the first remarkable thing I noticed about her. She smiled in an unguarded, hopeful type of way, but she wasn't naive. Jane was warm and self-possessed and dressed like a teacher.

"Hi," she said. I think I asked her how the drive was or something inane like that. It's the small talk that leads to intimacy — not strictly of the flesh, but of the mind. Truth is, I don't remember much of our initial talks other than that she was still in college studying business management to run the hotel her family owned back in Ireland. She laughed a lot about simple things and often for no reason at all. I think I didn't bother to remember much of the early bits because I figured we'd become casual lovers and we'd come to some sort of implicit and benign agreement and go on with our lives if things burned out.

We walked down to the Venice Pier and watched the waves crash against the concrete pillars. She told me about the shores in Ireland, but she didn't seem to miss it, or anything for that matter. Jane was not the type to dwell. She was unencumbered by old sentiment and had mastered the art of being in the moment. It would have been easy to mistake all of this for innocence.

We walked along the boardwalk towards Santa Monica and back again to the pier. She wanted to grab a drink, so we went to the Whaler. I shamelessly ordered some strewn-together variant of a pina colada. She ordered an Irish coffee. And a few drinks in, we were free to be ourselves; free to be gentle heathens, worshipping the present; free to say whatever we felt was true, so long as it was true when we said it. Her eyes were emerald green and ravenous in the honeyed hour right before sunset and I realized then that she was perfectly crazy and that we'd get along just fine.

As the evening came, I didn't find myself searching for things to talk about with Jane or looking to figure out the next thing to do. Everything was natural. She proposed one adventure after another. We drove to a park way up at the top of a neighborhood in Pacific Palisades on a street called Lachman Lane. It was nicknamed Top of the World because you could see the metropolis all spread out from the horizon to the sea, its scattered neon stars winking as if the city was keeping a secret that you could spend your whole life trying to understand. To the right, the Santa Monica ferris wheel marked the end of the continent. Beyond that a few solitary ships sailed through the night, floating on the pitch-black Pacific. A little further past the Ferris wheel, the Venice Pier jutted out into the sea. Further south, Ranchos Palos Verdes and Catalina Island rose out of the darkness. Ghostly-lit Mulholland drive snaked through the hills below the park and airplanes came and went from LAX, soaring beneath the blood moon. "That's where I live," she said pointing to Palos Verdes. To the far left, the downtown skyline loomed above the horizon.

She pointed out all the things she found beautiful and interesting and we started kissing and fooling around in the dark. We moved behind the privacy of a few bushes that scarcely covered us and undressed until she wore nothing but her heels and the moonlight. We got close; it was something in between making love and fucking. Her eyes were glittering emeralds in the dark and Jane became a living fantasy. But it was practiced. This was the second remarkable thing about her.

We carried on reveling in the dark even as high schoolers came to smoke their pot and drink just a few yards away at the Top of the World. Neither of us cared if they saw. I could have said anything and meant it on that mountain under those stars, all lit on fire from head to toe. The breeze carried the marijuana smoke over to us. We laid naked on our clothes watching the sky and listening to the kids laugh and drink. And we were as intimate as two people who don't love each other could be.

I was happy not working towards anything at all with her. It was nice just being. She wanted more than I was ready to give. Jane didn't want my confusion, but I think if you'd given her truth serum, she didn't want my certainty either. We saw each other a few more times after that. We stumbled along the sand-gritted streets of Venice and messed around in the streets like the world was our own little room. And then we snagged Ricky out of our apartment and strolled a couple hundred yards away to the rooftop bar of Hotel Erwin. We sat down at a table overlooking Dogtown. The boardwalk was desolate at night except for a skater or a drunk staggering here or there. The lights of Pacific Palisades and Malibu adorned the Santa Monica Mountains.

Jane asked Ricky about his life and he told her what brought him west, what he was doing, and what he loved to do. Music fed Ricky's soul. He could be great at it, or whatever he set his mind to, really. He had the heartbreaking gift of obsession. She asked him how we knew each other. How we'd become brothers through vibe. And we told her about growing up together, how we'd grown close through the years. We bragged about each other and were proud as two brothers. Girls have a way of trying to figure you out by looking at your friends. But I think she understood who I was. Ricky asked her if she had any girlfriends she could bring. She said they were all in Palos Verdes. The truth is, she was hesitant to pour her energy into anything that didn't yield a return. And I think she knew that all of it was just a moment, a lovely phase.

She came back with me to the apartment. Ricky went to bed. She also knew I didn't love her — except for that night. Some love is deep and seared into your soul; other love dries up like morning dew in the light of day. A breeze blew through the open window. She glowed in the candlelight and as it flickered, our shadows danced along the wall. Incense burned on the nightstand and her eyes were hungry for something. But the moment was the only thing I could afford to give

41

her. The couch was my bed, the room was my home. I collected the sun and the moon in those days and I knew she wanted more than memories.

We spent one last time together. She drove us to Malibu and we had lunch at Duke's after working up our appetites in bed. We sipped on Pina coladas and held hands at a table overlooking the ocean. She asked if I thought we were going anywhere. I told her I liked it the way it was. I was sure about two things with Jane: I was alright with letting her go and I'd miss these moments — just not enough. We didn't say much more and I could feel her melancholy shift to indifference as we watched the waves crash against the shore and recede once again. So it happened as I thought it would. There was an implicit and benign agreement to go on with our lives.

Chapter Three: Adulting

I eventually got hired as a link-building contractor for QuickRecruiter and Ricky would say that the reason he was able to keep his job was through company kickball. He insisted that it was just as important as the phone calls we'd make and the emails we'd send. His absurd theory turned out to be true.

We rode over to the kickball game and arrived early and at first, I didn't understand his intensity about it. He put on his headphones and listened to music and closed his eyes to meditate. We were the first ones to the field, but it wasn't long before an average-looking man strolled across the green to us.

"Hey Ricky," he said. It was John, our CEO. He greeted him like an old friend and by association, he gave me the same treatment. He was unconcerned with titles and had a different type of respect for Ricky than he did for the other employees. Shortly after, the rest of the team arrived — Brooke, a fiery brunette who cursed like a sailor; Andrea, a pixie-haired, tattooed sweetheart, who just wanted everybody in the world to be happy; Allison, who just wanted to be Andrea; Wes, a nice, lanky, easy-going guy; and a whole bunch of others I can't recall — all came at the same time.

At this point, I didn't have the full perspective of who John was. QuickRecruiter had raised $62 million in its series A round — more than any other company in L.A. history. Here, John was just a regular guy and that's all he wanted to be. All the soccer we grew up playing finally paid off in the most random of circumstances. Once the game started, Ricky and I were hitting home runs and giving our team hope even as we were getting our collective asses whooped by Hulu or some other tech juggernaut. The funniest bit of it was that John was quietly seething about losing, while putting on a good face for his employees in his one and only break during the week from work or family. John pulled Ricky and me aside after the game and asked as if we had more friends like us to play. "We need athletes," he said. The CEO of a multi-million dollar tech startup wanted us to recruit ringers to win recreational kickball.

Once it was over, Andrea and Allison invited us to go to Busby's, a little sports bar a couple miles from the fields. The Sunday tradition was that the employees would play kickball then get drunk at Busby's after. And who were we to break tradition? All the players from all the teams, distinguishable by their shirt colors, gathered in the back room where there was a long table set up for beer pong and drinking games and another room with pool tables and couches for kicking back.

We gathered around the table and played some sort of game where you try to bounce a ping pong ball into the cup of the person next to you. Or something like that. I was god awful and couldn't remember the rules. My talent has never been quickness of thought or tongue. I can appear quick through practice and obsession, but there was no way to cheat these rules. The real kicker was that every time you made a mistake, you had to drink the beer in the cup. Needless to say, I got shitfaced.

By that point I was gone. There are angry drunks, happy drunks, giggly drunks, horny drunks, and then there's the douchey networking drunk — that's who I was. The other reason for coming to L.A., a reason I failed to mention earlier, was that I was what you'd call an appreneur — a mashup of app creator and entrepreneur. During college, I noticed the kids would go to the library to study and to socialize. It wasn't one or the other or even an exclusive sort of thing. I also liked the simplicity and ease of use of Tinder. The swiping was as repetitive and mindless and equally addictive as eating French fries or potato chips.

My childhood friend Christian Chung and I were working to build a swipe-based app for finding study buddies on college campuses, a company we later brought Ricky into. The problem was none of us could code, so at that point in time we just had an idea. I thought maybe I'd find an answer out west, but again that wasn't my primary reason for skipping town.

The drunker I got, the more outwardly passionate I grew about StudyHubb, our Tinder for studying. I casually struck up conversations with people around the bar, knowing that everyone there more or less worked in tech. I treated every interaction like Shark Tank. In hindsight that shit is cringe worthy, but I was excited and optimistic and wanted to see StudyHubb become more than just an idea, a concept imprisoned in our minds.

I went around looking for our coveted coder, the one with the skill set to turn it into a reality. I offered equity because we had no money. But for someone making at minimum $80k a year, this wouldn't appeal to any of these guys. I was idealistic, thinking that surely someone would want a piece of a multi-million dollar business. Again, the problem was we had no business, no product, no proof, no leverage, and nothing to offer.

Ricky hung round Andrea, playing games and flirting with different girls at the table. That glint in his eye, the mischievous spark was flickering. Meanwhile, I succeeded at probably being the biggest douche at the bar.

After all the games were done and we'd had enough time to sober up, we headed back towards our place on South Venice Boulevard. I knew I hadn't smoked anything, but I saw a man in a wheelchair pushing himself as fast as he could along the side of the road. Behind him a cop car with its blue lights all lit up, slowly cruised in pursuit. I looked back and saw the man's face. He had determination written all over it and the sincerest belief that he could actually escape the cop in his wheelchair. And I think that man desperately spinning his wheels to elude the police officer about sums up the odds of becoming a star or something memorable in that wacky, wonderful, weird town called L.A. — but what else is there to do besides continue to push forward and spin our wheels?

Walking was my favorite thing to do alongside writing. Of course, I wouldn't list it as a hobby, but there's something about walking that gives you that extra time to absorb every detail. This habit fueled my prose. On days I didn't feel obligations pressing on me, I'd walk around the westside all along the coast. Sometimes right on up to Malibu. At night, I'd wander around Venice. I never got tired of stumbling on some new piece of graffiti, or the Pacific breeze blowing in between the rows of beach front houses, or the spontaneous conversations with free-spirited strangers. On any given night, the same bars and clubs would take on a different personality, changing with the vibe of their patrons.

Townhouse was usually more of a bohemian vibe, but on this particular night it took on a hint of bougie with the college crowd pouring in and out around the bums and the hipsters. I had gotten good at going out alone. The key is to possess an open mind, an open heart, a selective memory, and a dull sense of shame.

I started dancing my way through the people. My style was something between Mick Jagger and a chicken pecking for food with a little extra pelvic thrusting thrown in there for good measure. That goofiness is either off-putting or completely disarming. But that's also what helps you distinguish the people who take life and themselves too seriously from the people who have actually loved and lost and learned to laugh at their pain.

Downstairs in the basement, the college kids and the hipsters sat at their candlelit tables along the wall opposite to the bar. Several groups of people and couples danced together. Then I spotted a pretty girl in leather shorts dancing with one of her girlfriends. Her lips were voluptuous and painted red and she wore a constant grin -- almost a smirk like she was keeping a secret all to herself and reveling in her own mystery. We made eye contact and started mirroring each other's moves until that subtle currency of trust was built up just enough to get closer.

After a while, we started talk-yelling over the thump of the beat. We went through the who are you's, what's your name, where are you from — all the ordinary questions you have to ask to even start a sketch of a person. Her name was Susan and she was Vietnamese-American. She grew up in San Diego. She was adopted and had one brother, who in some fucked up way always seemed to want to challenge whether or not she deserved to have been chosen or was grateful for being adopted. I learned that last part later, anyway.

Susan would do this thing. Maybe it was unintentional. Probably not. She would squint her eyes as if she was searching you with them and then she'd open her mouth as if she was about to speak, but she'd pull back. It felt like she got off on being mysterious and leaving things unspoken. Her girlfriend Ansley would roam around the room getting free drinks for the both of them. Susan sipped hers and set them aside throughout the night. Ansley kept on drinking her whiskey sours and stumbling around looking to be loved in all the wrong places and all the wrong ways. She was pretty and full of insecurity.

Susan checked up on her friend one last time and grabbed my hand as we left the bar together. We strolled past a man playing guitar along the sidewalk and followed the breeze towards the beach, past the skate park until we were walking, shoes off in the sand. I always found that strange; that the beach would be so crowded during the day and then at night when the moon made the tide dance and the ocean shimmer and the Santa Monica Ferris Wheel changed colors up the shore, it was desolate. We had the beach and the night to ourselves and we held hands and talked about simple things. She went to college with Ansley in San Luis Obispo and then they'd worked their way down to Santa Barbara and now they'd come to Los Angeles. For what? I don't think she knew. But her confusion added to her intrigue. She didn't have the desperation of someone who had to work to make ends meet. It was obvious she came from money and was drawn to money.

Everything was fluid, but there was a hint of hesitation behind her words and actions; something she wanted to tell me and to keep to herself at the same time. Her laughter started off sweet and pure before it trailed off with a touch of hurt. I didn't press or care to know. I had my suspicions, but I let that moment simply be what it was. We walked back towards the bars and Susan met back up with Ansley and we hugged good night. Sometimes you know it'll be the last time you see someone, sure as fact. Other times, there's a magnetism or a gravity like your souls are tethered. You cannot say how long you'll be in each other's lives, but you can be sure that you will know each other for as long as the universe intends for you to.

She picked me up at the place on 31 South Venice Boulevard that next night. She came in and I introduced her to Ricky. I didn't tell her I was essentially couch-crashing for the long haul. The incense was burning and she seemed to like the modesty of the place. She thought our setup was unassuming, but really I was just broke. We left for 1544 Lachman Lane, cruising through the night along Pacific Coast Highway.

The Malibu beachfront homes, the ferris wheel, the scattered shiplights on the ocean; I'd dreamt of these things on the east coast and now I was here with a beautiful stranger driving up the Pacific Palisades hills, climbing our way up to heaven.

Susan parked her car in the cul de sac at the top of the neighborhood. "Is this what you wanted to show me?" No, not this. Not these houses. I led her to cinder block steps and stayed behind her. The hill was steep, but she grabbed onto the fence to the most extravagant, perfectly Los Angeles home you could imagine. It had a platform in the backyard for gazing over the city and feeling like the whole thing was yours. Supposedly, Kobe Bryant had lived there a few years back.

We sat down and just watched. It moved her. I could feel it. And L.A. just glittered as it always does, more impressively than the stars. At the sight of it, you'd swear half the angels dropped out of heaven to shine on earth instead. I reached over and held her hand and she rubbed her thumb on mine as a subtle gesture of reassurance. Still she was doing that thing where she had something to say, but kept swallowing the truth. Until she broke. "I have a boyfriend." I didn't know her well, but it was a little sad to hear. "I mean, it's complicated," she said. "He cheated on me." Really, my best advice to anyone else is to flee from confused people. It's far easier to give advice anyway, and I have a tendency, for better or worse, of seeing how life plays out. It also would have been the decent thing to leave her alone then and there. All signs pointed towards retreat. But I figured he was a stranger and a cheater at that, so if it somehow got around to him, it would be cosmic justice, karma, even. "How long have you been together?" I asked. "Almost three years," she replied. "But I'm not sure what I'm gonna do." She said plenty of things like this to string me along. And it worked. Hope is a double-edged sword — it's the flicker in your soul that guides you to better days. It's also the first step to tripping over your feelings and impaling yourself on disappointment.

We kept holding hands as we talked, but the vibe was different. Now, the phantom of a stranger loomed and she was remotely distant. It felt doomed. And from that, I grew a little desperate because I actually cared about the outcome. For her, I was a sort of secret, petty revenge, an anesthesia for her bitterness. Just a line she could skirt without feeling as if she'd cheated, or done anything wrong. It was that look she had when she'd gaze off. I recognized it from those the times I'd find myself doing the same, peering through space at Isabella with all the dreamy memories flooding in. She was bleary-eyed and broken. Maybe some part of me empathized with her. Maybe I was attracted to that specific type of pain; that somehow we could help each other empty out the skeletons in our closets and banish our ghosts.

At the peak of my personal dilemma, a naked twenty-something man and a fully-clothed woman came trudging up the trail and decided to sit down with us. He wore nothing but a red bandana and tennis shoes and carried something in his hands as he proudly displayed his acorn-sized penis for all to see. The girl had fake lips, but besides that was decently attractive and normal-seeming compared to her companion for the night. "Can we join ya?" he asked. "Yeah, man." We acted like it wasn't a thing at all to greet strangers in the nude. Two minutes into the conversation with our whacky new acquaintances, the girl volunteered the fact that she was not in a relationship with him and that it was actually their first time meeting. "Tinder date," she said to distance herself from him. He had a bottle of wine and a joint and he lit it. He took a hit and held it out for us. I took a hit and passed it to Susan who did the same. The girl had a long drink from the wine bottle as if she was trying to drown out the memory of the acorn-tipped penis.

We followed her so that we were a little high and a little tipsy after a few rotations around our circle.

"So how do you two know each other?" she asked. "We met a couple nights ago actually," Susan answered. The girl was prodding to see what her options were. She had gotten dolled up for the date only for her night to end up like this. She just wanted to be seen. The girl not so subtly slid over next to me. "So you're not together?" I looked over at Susan to get a hint at how to answer the question. "We're getting to know each other," I said, "but I'm interested in her."

The truth is, in love, mystery is an aphrodisiac. In war, you don't give away your position too early or you die. Voltaire said, the secret to being boring is to say everything. He was right. I was no longer the stranger she met in the basement of Townhouse. She knew she could have me there until she figured out what she wanted to do. And that's just too easy. We left the nudist and the girl shortly after and called it a night.

We had a few more nights like that; nights when she couldn't sleep. I didn't sleep well either. But for different reasons. She'd pick me up and we'd go get 24-hour Korean barbeque at Hodori. We'd drive around. We'd talk. We'd do whatever we could not to be alone with ourselves. I had a theory that she was different enough to numb the quiet and steady longing that was calling me back home. In place of innocence, she was calculating. But that appealed to the part of me that wanted to climb. Maybe I had this vision of us finding our way together because we were both a little lost. We stayed friends for a while, but that initial flame died down.

Chapter Four: Santa Monica

Ricky and I needed to move. The lease was running out. Really, it was his choice where we'd go. He was still paying the bulk of the rent. He found a two-bedroom spot in Santa Monica on 5th and Bay. It was close to Main Street, just a few blocks up from the beach, and it was a stone's throw away from the QuickRecruiter headquarters. We checked it out and ended up moving into it in short order. I missed our Venice pad right away. The new place was nicer and I finally had a bed instead of carrying on like a bum, but in Cali terms, the vibe wasn't right. Sometimes you know how fortunate you are to even be in a certain situation, so that's what I focused on. My heart just didn't agree for whatever reason. As soon as we got settled in, I went to Main Street with a stack of resumes to see if my luck would be any better. I handed one into an Irish pub even though I had no bartending experience, another to a crystal shop despite not knowing or giving a damn about that woo woo mystical mumbo jumbo, and another to an ice cream shop — none of which were my ideal targets, but as the joke goes, if you tell someone you're an actor or an actress in L.A. the proper response is, "Which restaurant do you work at?" I figure the same joke could be made about writers and novelists.

Then I walked into Max Studio's, a women's retail clothing store. Again, not my ideal choice or fit, but a job's a job. The first person I spoke to was a sweet guy named Todd. He was the manager. He was curious why I wanted to work there. As he put it, I was the only straight male who'd ever come to apply. I told him bluntly that I needed to make some money to which he asked if I knew anything about women's clothing. No, of course I didn't. But I'm willing and ready to learn, I said. And that was that. I was hired on the spot and would start the next day. I kept looking for other jobs to work in addition to the online music startup, QuickRecruiter, and Max Studios. I noticed a contemporary art gallery with a marble sculpture of a man holding an iPhone up to take a selfie. The door was wide open. At first it seemed nobody was around, which was a bit strange considering the exorbitantly priced artwork would be unattended. Then I caught a whiff of marijuana and followed it up a wooden ramp, where two men sat at a desk clearly stoned off their asses. They looked at me with red-eyes and flashed two satisfied grins. Immediately, it was clear that they had achieved what they wanted in life. Not that that's a bad thing at all. It's simply to say that by all appearances they'd attained stoner nirvana through mastering contentedness. Both of them were about six foot five. One was handsome and wore a hat and a plaid shirt. He was some strangely cool fusion of a surfer and a lumberjack and a hipster. The other had a beard and a more discerning eye. "Hey, man," said the bearded one. "How can I help?"

"I'm looking for a job," I said. "Do you know Mailchimp?" No. Do you know...no. Do you know...no. I realized then how little I knew. "You're hired," he said, "when can you start?" So now I had four part-time jobs. Not a single full-time gig, but I was slowly moving up in the big ol' world. Five days a week I worked at Max Studios. Two days at Axiom, the art gallery. In the mornings before work I sent emails and made calls for QuickRecruiter and at night I curated content for Music Aficionado. The most serious part of job was ensuring that the clothing was spaced out evenly on the hangers throughout the store as customers browsed for what they wanted. Other than that, we just stood around and had to appear busy for the cameras the bosses supposedly watched. It's really in those moments when the existential crisis arises again — is this my fate? Is this the consolation prize for losing out on your life's purpose? Death by retail?

The art gallery gig was alright and the bosses paid generously. We'd smoke their weed on the back patio. They'd sing and play guitar while nobody was around. The only reason for the storefront was for the occasional sale, but more so to showcase the art in a nice enough area with some prestige rather than stowing it away in a warehouse and risking unnecessary damages. Every other week the bosses were in Miami or the Hamptons or Shanghai at a high end art festival, where the one percenters and the super elite flocked to find even a single piece to add to their collections. When they were around, my main responsibility was to handle the artwork as if my life depended on it, to wax off any scratches the pieces may have gotten during shipping, and to run errands for them. Somehow my first full day on the job I went to get a certain type of paint using the jefe's truck. I got the wrong type of paint, blew a tire, and temporarily lost the company credit card while filling the tire with air before finding it in the gas station parking lot. Fortunately, they liked me so I kept the job, but it wasn't the smooth start I'd hoped for.

Susan called me a few nights after I'd gotten all mixed up and busy with the jobs, head spinning, wondering about life. She asked me if she could pick me up just as she did when I lived in Venice. But something changed. Something was different now. She was hurting, but she'd made up her mind — even if she didn't know it yet. "Come get food with me," she'd text at 2 in the morning. And I was there. We'd drive through the night listening to Honne, a sort of downbeat new age R&B. The singer's voice was sleepy like the hours we cruised around the city. She wanted to talk about her ex. I wanted to talk about mine, but I couldn't. Instead, I just knew we were the same. So there we were at 2 and 3 in the morning eating 24-hour Korean barbeque at Hodori. That became our sad, exciting little ritual.

My uncle's leukemia was spiraling out of control back home. I wanted to go back to see him, but my parents told me there was nothing that could be done. I was working four part-time jobs and still barely saving any money. But I knew I was fortunate and had it far better than most. My mind knew that, at least. I found myself thinking about Isabella more and more. I walked along the shore in the early morning and collected small bits of sea glass near the Santa Monica Pier; blues, greens, oranges, reds — all worn down by the salt and the tide. I thought she'd like them. I placed them inside a tequila bottle with lavender I'd picked from a garden on our street.

My birthday crept up. After 21, they all feel more or less the same with new responsibilities packed on. Diego, my teammate and friend from college, came out to visit me for his spring break and to celebrate his birthday, which was three days from my own. To him, California represented an all-you-can-smoke buffet of marijuana — his American Dream. The moment we picked him up from the airport he wanted to know where we could get weed. Out there I didn't have a dealer in my phone. "The skatepark," I said. "That's your best bet." We ran into dead ends there, mostly because it's not the brightest idea to go asking strangers for drugs, and if my memory serves me correctly, you need a California driver's license to buy from the dispensaries. Ricky had a little extra weed, so he hooked him up. "Sup, boyo," Diego would say. He had the thickest Spanish accent. He'd been in the states for about five years in Tennessee and Georgia. I would always wonder why someone would leave Madrid and the Mediterranean with its beautiful women and tapas for the rural south, but the pull of wanderlust is strong; the promise of Somewhere Else.

Diego was basically the Cookie Monster, but instead of cookies, he needed a steady supply of weed. We went to the beach to kick the soccer ball around. Vera, a girl from Tinder, said she'd bring a friend with her. Two hours later, she came alone from Van Nuys, which is a 405-L.A. traffic eternity away. Diego and I juggled the ball back and forth and passed it to her. Vera was quiet and unassuming. She was pretty, but she hadn't been pursued hard in her entire life. After a while Diego decided to walk back to the apartment to smoke more with Ricky. Vera and I stayed behind, walking the beach. I learned she wanted to be a radiologist and was in a sorority and she was Guatemalan and liked going to concerts. And also that we had nothing in common besides the fact that we both enjoyed sex more than the average person. Our conversation devolved into a theoretical game of scenarios. We talked some more and then the date, if it was that, ended ordinarily.

That night I tried to get Diego to go out, but he was too stoned. During most of his visit I had to work at Max Studios shifting clothes hangers around and sweeping the floors. My coworker Lizzy was the one thing I liked about going to work there. Her ex-boyfriend Chaz would come around. He'd always pretend to be her brother, and she pretended to be annoyed by him, but the love and whatever they'd had was all still intact. He was a cool guy. She would brag about him, talking about how he got paid to travel the world as a model. I'd wait till Happy Hour to take my breaks, so I could get a big plate of calamari for five dollars at Areal, where I'd sit outside and listen to the guitarists play acoustic sets. But when Chaz was around, we'd go to an Irish pub a few doors down and drink a couple beers and grab a burger and talk about dreams and women.

Diego's second night in town, Lizzy had a friend, a petite and pretty redhead from Dallas named Hillary come visit her. Hillary wore designer pants, designer clothes, designer earrings, designer everything. I was somewhat surprised considering Lizzy didn't strike me as the bougie type and I wouldn't think that would be her crowd of choice. But her dad, as it turns out, had some type of plumbing empire back in Dallas and was good pals with Mark Cuban. She had a pattern of choosing the path with the most resistance and she lived in a state of constant rebellion, and made it all look damn good.

As work was closing up, Lizzy invited me to go with her to Busbee's, the same neighborhood bar Ricky and I frequented with the QuickRecruiter kickball teammates. Lizzy didn't really have any interest in me, so I knew Hillary was behind the invite. I asked if Diego could come along. We went to my place and picked him up. The bar was bustling with energy. Most of the patrons were white collar workers looking to blow off steam.

Lizzy introduced me to her friend Benjamin. He'd been drinking and starting off telling me how handsome I was. Meanwhile, Diego swaggered off into the crowded bar, talking to any girl he could find. His confidence came and went in streaks. In college, there was a night he snagged a bottle of tequila from the bar on Main Street and then had sex with a girl in the girl's bathroom stall of a Mellow Mushroom pizza restaurant. Drunk Diego was a hurricane, the Tasmanian Devil cartoon come to life. In the meantime, Benjamin was describing the plot of his novel about a gay detective, who falls in love with his fellow detective, who incidentally ends up on a hunt for a gay serial killer, who targets gay prostitutes. Lizzy took interest in a guy selling cigarettes in the smoking section. He didn't know or seem to care. That always seems to do the trick — the not caring part. At least, for stoking curiosity. Everything is an exchange of values and there's an underlying assumption that the disinterested have more value. Of course, nobody will openly admit to this, but it's a simple truth.

Lizzy grew bored with the cigarette guy right as he started to realize he had a chance to get with her. She floated off into the night, into another part of the bar, leaving him in a daze and a soft cloud of her perfume. Somehow, we wound up talking, which gave me an excuse to pardon myself from the conversation about the homoerotic Sherlock Holmes and Watson. "Where you from?" Atlanta, I said. "No shit," he said, "me too. What part?" Marietta. No fucking way. Yeah.

"My name's Dan," he said.

"Anthony."

"What brought you out here?"

"Writing, business, the girls, the beach," I told him. "How about you?"

"I'm a filmmaker and a comedian," he said. "You with that girl?"

"Nah, man," I said. "I think she's feeling you, though."

"You wanna be?"

"Definitely wouldn't mind," I said. "But I don't have my life together at all."

"How old are you?"

"23."

"Dude, I'm 32 and I'm still figuring it out. Everyone's pretending out here. We're all just kids playing adults."

Dan was just a small character in the story of my life, but sometimes a stranger speaks directly to the things on your heart. He made Atlanta feel just for a moment like it was just a short ride away. He didn't seem to mind the uncertainty of a journey to nowhere. The excitement for him was in the bumps along the way and the act of doing. He was comfortable in his own skin. I wasn't yet.

Lizzy was able to be a lot of things at once, things that didn't seem to go together — like how she made drunken wobbling look graceful as we left the bar, like how she was a romantic, pill-popping cokehead party girl, who dreamed of white houses and picket fences and babies and staying out until twilight and getting high in the night. And it was all her; the sweetness, the hunger, the recklessness. We found Hillary and Diego and after listening to me go on about the Top of the World, they let me talk them into driving there.

"What is this place?" they asked. "It looks like a neighborhood."

"You just walk up these steps for a few feet and it's at the top..."

"It's cold," Lizzy said.

"Yeah, this feels like a bad idea."

We stayed up there for a few minutes passing a joint before they got tired and bored and cold and were over it. I wanted them to see it and to feel it. That's some of my selfishness — it translates poorly to love too; wanting to give the love you want to give and not the love they need. I always wanted to share the world and I don't understand people who don't care to feast on its sights and smells and all the things that are too great for money to buy. Doesn't it matter that sunsets are like snowflakes? No two are just the same. Doesn't it matter what the flowers smell like?

Diego stayed a few more days. We smoked weed and played video games and did all the things he was doing in college. And then he was off again. The past and the future started to distinguish themselves from one another.

I kept working the retail job until my existential crisis boiled over. I didn't show up to work at Max Studios when I was scheduled or ever again after that. I was pretty much the epitome of all the worst millennial stereotypes at that point, but I was losing my sanity centimeter by centimeter, hanger by hanger.

It had been about a month since I last saw Susan. She texted me one afternoon to invite me to a Founder Meets Funder event at a co-working space for entrepreneurs to pitch their startups to investors. She was tending bar and got me in for free and somehow talked them into letting me be one of the ten companies to pitch. I was anxiously waiting outside in the line to get in, not knowing what to expect. That's where I met Brad. He looked seventeen or eighteen years old with dark silky hair that stood up and alabaster skin and he exuded a quiet, but powerful confidence.

"Have you been to one of these before?" I asked.

"Oh, yeah," he said. "This your first time?"

"Yeah, I'm a little nervous, but excited."

"Don't be," he said. "I'm Brad, by the way."

"Anthony. What do you do Brad?"

"I started an app called Earigami. Think Snapchat but for audio," he said.

He pulled his phone out and demonstrated Earigami.

"These filters change the style of your voice just like Snapchat does for pics."

His prototype was beautiful."

"What do you do?"

"I have a mobile app called StudyHubb. It's kind of like Tinder but for finding study buddies. You swipe right on someone you want to study with and they do the same. So if both people swipe right, to show that it's mutual, we match you, and you can message them."

"Oh, cool," he said. "Can I see it?"

"Ah, see that's the thing," I said. "It's not really to market or even a minimally viable product."

I was a little embarrassed truthfully. You always hear people say fake it till you make it, but I felt like I was in a perpetual cycle of faking it. Imposter syndrome.

"That's alright," said Brad. "You have to start somewhere; you know? The big thing is that you can sell yourself. Investors invest in people. The idea is secondary. It comes down to whether or not they like you and trust you enough to give you money."

The doormen opened up the building and all of the entrepreneurs came flooding into the startup campus full of hope and varying degrees of desire to change the world. The investors were mostly easy to pick out of the crowd. There was a certain calculated casualness to them, an air that many had come to window shop. Others wanted to be sold.

Susan worked the bar and anyone who visited her. She wore a skintight dress and heels and bright red lipstick. She was dressed to climb to the stars. I went to see her before everyone got settled into their seats for the presentations.

"This is something," I told her. "Thank you for getting me in."

"Just remember me when you blow up," she said. "I do like fancy things. No shame."

"Same to you," I said. "The remembering part."

There was a pause. The old cadence was off.

"Can I get you something to drink? It might help with the nerves."

"You can tell?"

"I know you, Anthony."

A couple of well-dressed entrepreneurs came up to order drinks.

"How have you been?"

"Good," she said. "Be right back."

She poured them their drinks and one by one she was swarmed with orders. I left to mingle with the other attendees, excited by the possibility that someone in the room could help bring my idea to life. In each conversation circle I joined the theme was the same — the ideas were all already out there in the market. At first, this was discouraging, but I tried to frame my imaginary app as an innovation hiding in plain sight. You're either a visionary, delusional, or you weren't delusional long enough to become a visionary — you don't know till later. I listened more than I spoke.

Then Brad found me in the crowd, flanked by an attractive, slightly inebriated blonde with big, bright ravenous blue eyes and an intellectual property lawyer, who wore a near constant smirk.

"Delilah, this is my new friend Anthony," Brad said. "Anthony, this is Delilah."

"What's your thing?" she slurred.

"StudyHubb," I said. "It's like Tinder but for finding study buddies."

"Study fuck," she laughed. "Study buddies...right."

I turned my shoulder to her, facing Brad.

"I'm just kidding," said Delilah. "I'm blunt, but seriously, I think StudyHubb...StudyHubb is it right?"

I nodded.

"Yeah, I think StudyHubb is an interesting idea," she said. "But call it like it is. Sex sells."

"Anthony, StudyHubb is a great idea," Brad added. "It'll help a lot of students. Hell, I would've used it in school."

"What do you do, Delilah?" I asked.

"I'm a connector," she said. "I bring the right people together."

Delilah gently pulled a stocky, bald-headed guy with gauges, and a well-kept beard and mustache into our little circle.

"Who are you?" she asked him with her face close enough for him to smell the champagne on her breath.

He pretended not to like her sudden attention.

Tanner Wilde," he said cooly. "I run an eco-friendly collective for artists, acrobats and entrepreneurs with green products."

"I like you, Tanner," she said. "We're going to be good friends. This is Brad, that's Frank and this is Anthony. He started Study Fuck. It's for students to find fuck buddies."

"No," I interjected. "It's an app for students to find study buddies."

"I'm a fan of your app. That's a great elevator pitch and I'm also all about the vibe, man. I can tell you're hungry. I dig that," he said.

"Thank you," I said. "I'd like to stay connected, Tanner. Have you met Brad, too? He's got an app called Earigami. It's like Snapchat but for audio."

"That's dope. Brad it's awesome to meet you," he said.

"Likewise, Tanner."

Even Delilah meant well. She was searching for family in her own way, which at that particular moment manifested itself as belligerence. She was jaded, but I would come to call her a friend and a few years later she'd go on to get married and have a daughter.

An announcement came over the mic telling everyone to be seated for Founder Meets Funder. We fell into a hush and sat where we could find open seats. I was sweating bullets nervous, but the possibility of something special coming out of that night, got me over myself. Most of the pitches are a blur to me now except for Brad's Earigami and these two brilliant women, who demonstrated their website. It was beautifully designed, geared towards millennials and already generating millions of dollars already through online guides about dating and all types of social media-suited content. Investors pounced on them after they were done speaking.

Number 10, StudyHubb was called. I got up on the stage, surveyed the room and started speaking about what I believed was true, pushing aside the concern that I'd sound utterly delusional.

"StudyHubb is a swipe-based mobile app helping students find study buddies," I said. "Currently, there isn't really a cool, fun, casual edtech platform for students to make connections, but our academic social network with Tinder-like interfaces, is the perfect ice-breaker. With over 20 million college students in the U.S. alone, StudyHubb has plenty of room to scale by following Tinder's blueprint. The best part is that the market replenishes every four years. Funding would be used for development costs and to pay for a nationwide campus ambassador program."

Part of me thought someone, just one person in the crowd would be impressed, but they'd heard it before. The wantrepreneur talking about the billion-dollar startup unicorn. After all the pitches were over, I reconvened with Brad, Frank, Delilah and Tanner and a Spanish woman who ran her company out of the coworking space. Her name was Estrella and she had a women's exercise app.

Susan tapped me on the shoulder. She was smiling ear to ear.

"This is my friend, Anthony," she said.

"Anthony, this is Brian Kim and his business partner Mykel."

Both men were casually dressed. Their eyes were gentle and kind in a practiced sort of way.

"Susan has said great things about you," said Mykel. "I'd love to hear what you do as would my associate and friend."

I was excited to have anyone's interest in StudyHubb. After a long conversation, it turned out that they were masquerading as investors when, in fact, their company was a loan office. The night was mostly fruitless, but meeting Brad, Tanner and even stumbling drunk Delilah, the hot mess she was, were all blessings. In a world of critics and doubters, creators encourage each other's wonderful delusions. As I was leaving, Susan walked up the sidewalk of the dim lit street with a couple of guys who'd worked the door. She gave a quick wave back and disappeared around the corner.

Chapter Five: Old Ghosts and New Friends

The loneliness was as steady as the women who came in and out of my life. Every other night I went out. After a few drinks, I'd see Isabella, my beautiful ghost, haunting the shadows. Vera was sweet and we kept spending time together, but we both knew that it had gone as far as it ever would. We had an arrangement of the flesh but our souls never got together.

I took the boardwalk from Santa Monica down to Venice. Most nights I didn't know what I was looking for other than something new to write about. Canal Club was overcrowded with the drunk college crowd spilling onto the sidewalk. The line to James Beach was short, so I made a stop there. Still, the frat boys and the sorority girls rotated from one room to another in packs. I ordered a jack and coke and danced my way into the middle of a circle of 30-something girlfriends, who were either having a divorce party or a bachelorette party. I danced with a brunette in white pants. That's all I remember about her. That, and she was sweet and easy conversation. After a while I pardoned myself from their group before I could overstay my welcome and become the uninvited creep who lingers too long.

I sat in a booth drinking my whiskey and watching the room stir. I liked the people who were in it. Really in it and nowhere else. Like the blonde in the romper, smiling and dancing and laughing. By nature, I'm actually shy and maybe a little scared of everything, but when I see something that looks like fun I just want to play with it. I walked up to her and danced near her and we started playing off each other's moves, if you'd call them that. Then I grabbed her hand and we danced face-to-face close. Her name was Kathy. She graduated from UCLA and worked for Coca-Cola in sales and she stared.

We kissed and she stared some more. And we were immediately out of things to talk about, but it was cool. After that night we kept hanging out long enough for me to see the scar on her stomach she got from a piece of hot macaroni falling on her after her mom let her cook unattended as a three-year old. I'm still baffled by the physics and how the scar was perfectly macaroni-shaped. But we just wouldn't work and it wasn't for any fault of hers besides the fact that she wasn't someone I'd already loved. And it's just like that. Half of us are stuck looking at stars that burned out eons ago. We love the dead ones all the same.

I was in college when I met Isabella. She was kind and innocent and she asked questions. She was curious and smart and wildly intuitive and I fell deeply in love with her before I knew what to do with it. On our first date I turned on bachata in the car and she thought that it was to impress her. We kissed in the movie theater and I could feel the chills on her skin and she was warm. Everything was warm with her. Warm like being wine drunk. Warm like sunflowers. Warm like candlelight. Eventually, we made love. I was her first. She was my first love. I can say that much. And the girl who went to the chapel to pray on her own was mine. She trusted me with her heart and her soul, but I was reckless with it. We were on and off again. Fiercely together and fiercely apart. And then a few years later, I got her pregnant. We were both nervous for our own reasons, but we were also excited to have a baby. She took her vitamins and did everything you're supposed to do when you're expecting.

And then Isabella called me one morning. She was crying. "I think something's wrong," she said. "I'm bleeding." I drove as quickly as I could to pick her up. Her white pants were red from all the blood.

We pulled up to the emergency room. I grabbed a wheelchair and wheeled her in. We were supposed to find out the sex in a week, but we already knew he was a boy. We could feel it. And then, we knew he was gone before he'd arrived. But he was far enough along that she still had to deliver him. We held him in a paper towel and we wept and we held each other and they sent us off with a blue teddy bear for comfort after the night was done. We had given him my father's first name and her father's first name as his middle name and that's what he was and is to us. He was our son even as the doctor told us, "You can have another."

I say all this because I missed her like hell. All the memories of the good, the bad and the heart-wrenching were on my mind. I was walking along the beach at sunset when all the parents were done with work for the day and had brought their kids to play in the sand. I saw a mother holding her little boy's hands to help him stand upright as he gave a toothy grin. I saw a little boy's hand clasped around his father's pinky giggling as the water rushed over his tiny toes. I dreamed with my eyes open. I watched the parents and their children in sepia tone with golden light flowing around them and then I saw my son at a tender age he never reached, just old enough to stand. He wrapped his hand around my pinky and ring finger and we walked until it was time for him to go again. And I cried, but they weren't sad tears this time.

When it comes to certain things, you don't get closure; there's none to be had. I've never been one to take solace in the idea that everything happens for a reason. No, things just happen and we do what we can to keep moving with the pace of the earth.

I started floating more. Not like a butterfly. More like a plastic bag, picked up and carried whichever way the wind was compelled to take me. I was floating like that, wandering in the sunshine on a grassy park near the Santa Monica Pier when I saw a long-legged woman taking pictures of flowers blooming from succulents. She was smiling to herself and looked like she was humming. And she did float like a butterfly.

I walked up to her and started to ask her about her photography. Sometimes that would have just been a line, an easy conversation starter, but she looked happy and I wanted to know her secret. If she had one, or many. Her name was Helen. She was living with her grandma between jobs and she was an actress and a painter and a writer and a singer, she said. She had nowhere to be and nothing to do, but she liked the idea of everything and every suggestion. So we walked down past the pier along the shore to Malibu.

Helen was over thirty and she talked on and on about being an actress. I couldn't help, but feel sad for her in the way you do for a horse with a broken leg because all that can be done is to shoot it in the head. Then I felt a tinge of self-pity because I was like her with my imaginary app and my imaginary novel and I wondered if I was actually the broken-legged horse that ought to be shot in the head. We went bowling at an alley near my apartment that night and then we came back and had hollow sex because neither of us had the answer we both thought the other might. It was time to move again.

The timing was good. The little inkling of gypsy in Ricky was itching to go somewhere else again. He had a place in mind — an apartment complex he'd looked at when he was dating the Spanish girl he'd originally moved out there with. We drove over to Marina Del Rey, which was right on the other side of Venice opposite to Santa Monica. It was quieter and overshadowed by the glitzier parts of L.A. The Mariner's Village apartments we came to look at were relics in comparison to the complexes around them. They'd been built in the seventies and had brown wooden exteriors. Tiny man-made waterfalls and streams flowed around the apartments, giving the feel of an amusement park and there was a large wooden tower about seven stories tall above the complex. Danny, one of the managers, toured us around the property. The apartment we were looking at had a fireplace, two bedrooms, a balcony, a living room and a kitchen. The clubhouse had a library, a 24-hour gym and sauna and hot tubs. There were three pools on the property and the backside of it looked out into the marina. Sailboats and yachts passed through at all hours of the day.

"Yeah, we'll do it," Ricky said. "What's next, Danny?"

By the afternoon, we'd signed all the paperwork and committed to the place for a year. Ricky and I took the stairs up to the top of the tower and peered in every direction. From there you could see the Santa Monica Mountains, the ferris wheel, Venice Beach, LMU, Palos Verdes, Catalina Island way off in the distance, the sailboats gliding on the ocean and the city in the other direction.

"This is perfect," I said.

"It really is, man," Ricky replied. "I'm gonna make music here."

It was a fresh start and another chance to leave our baggage behind. We moved our stuff in over the course of two trips to the old apartment. Mine only took one because I hadn't brought much with me from Georgia to begin with. My room connected to the balcony, so I heard the rushing water and if I left the screen door open I could enjoy the breeze blowing in and out. I bought a mattress and set it on the floor and I had a rock salt lamp, which glowed a sunset pink, and I had my granddad's old pool cue from his Nashville days as a big shot in the country music business and *the Eagles* "Hotel California" vinyl Ricky had gotten me. And I had a small pile of books in the corner and clothes in my closet. That was my setup and all I needed. I didn't get a bedframe and I had no plans to. If something was borderline non-essential I didn't need it.

After we were all moved in and we'd gone grocery shopping, I took off my shoes, put my headphones in, hopped over the balcony railing and went for a run down the sidewalk. Barefoot, shirtless. I felt closer to the world that way like its energy was wrapping around and I was one of its animals, mindless and at peace, free of expectations. I listened to "Lying Eyes" and "Hotel California" as I ran from the jetty of the marina down past the Venice Pier. I sat breathless and watched the sunset from the rocks. The sea sprayed me as the waves crashed against the boulders. The setting sun seemed to confirm the conclusion of one chapter and the sea mist baptised me for the road ahead.

Ricky and I were working out that first weekend there and we used the sauna afterwards to recover. We'd talk about dreams and goals and life in there. Something about the choice to suffer brings men together like the Native peoples in their sweat lodges long before saunas were around for alcoholics to detox. Speaking of alcoholics, that's where we met R.J. He came in sniffling, on edge, red-faced and hungover. R.J. was a bulky guy with dark slicked back hair and stubbly facial hair. He grinned.

"What's up, cousin?" he said.

We got to talking. I'd ask about him. He'd ask about me. It was give and take and we vibed straight away. He liked Ricky, too. R.J. claimed to be a marketing maven, a film producer and a connector. Everyone in L.A. is a connector or an influencer or an actor or a something. He was from San Diego and looked about forty. He had a scar and steel rods in his leg — the result of ending up on the wrong side of a brawl back in college at Colorado State. It was over a futon or something equally ridiculous. After we'd been talking for a few minutes, a couple of voices echoed in the locker room right outside of the sauna — a woman's voice and two men, which was obviously a bit unexpected in the men's locker room.

"Tell them I'm your guest here," R.J. said nervously.

"Why?"

"Some dumb stuff from a while back," he said. "Trust me. She's an uptight bitch."

"Who?"

"Trust, cousin," he said. "Explain in a sec."

Two of the property security guards burst into the sauna with a blonde woman I recognized as one of the property managers behind them.

"I'm with them," R.J. said nervously. "Right, cousin?"

"Yeah, he's my guest," I said.

"He's not supposed to be here," said the manager.

"Alright, I'm leaving."

"Yeah, you are," she added.

R.J. muttered as they escorted him out.

"I'll text you, cousin," he yelled back.

"Sounds good," I said. "See you later, R.J."

R.J. was a sketchy guy. You had to take everything he said and did with a grain of salt, but he had this frenetic exuberance about him. He was charismatic enough that I didn't even mind the fact that he was probably lying about many things, if not everything he said. Los Angeles is the land of make believe and to really belong, you have to participate. We were all pretending to be something to whatever degree our consciences and our acting allowed us to. I knew I'd be seeing R.J. again.

I kept working for QuickRecruiter, but now I was officially hired as a contractor instead of getting paid through Ricky for the work I'd helped him with. I was still working the Music Aficionado job as a content curator, but I needed to make more money. So I started applying online. I looked for job titles with writer in it. Copywriting jobs kept popping up. There weren't as many as you'd think there'd be in a city as big as L.A. I hadn't heard of copywriting back then, but I looked it up.

The act of writing text for the purpose of advertising or other forms of marketing.

I liked the idea of that. I imagined the job being like something straight out of *Mad Men*. BeachHead Creative was hiring. It was one of the only positions that I felt I had all the skills to do well at. I applied and received an email a few days later requesting a writing sample. I submitted it and was asked to come in for an in-person interview. Law of attraction. Power of positive thinking. Whatever you want to call it — I had actually given it up. In fact, I didn't really expect to hear anything back when I sent in my resume.

I Ubered to their office in Calabasas. We took PCH along Malibu and took a right onto Topanga Canyon. The road snaked through mountains and canyons with large boulders and layers of massive rock stacked diagonally like sheets of paper. We passed by whimsically painted wooden houses nestled at the base of the hills. I wondered how many musicians and actors had retreated to the area to create. It was quieter, shadier and hidden from the noise with crooked trees and little streams flowing randomly here and there. The road twisted and turned higher and higher into the mountains until we were out of the canyons and looking over the San Fernando Valley, the congested capital of the porn industry.

A few minutes later, we pulled up to a small office building. I got out and went right up to the door and let myself in. I took the elevator to the second floor to be interviewed. The office was brightly lit and every employee was fit besides a couple of the web designers. I sat down on a couch to wait. A few moments later, an attractive dirty-blonde with smart blue eyes came over to me.

"Anthony?"

"Yes, you must be..."

"Kennedy," she said. "From the emails."

"It's a pleasure to meet you, Kennedy."

I was noticing a pattern in their hiring decisions pretty quickly. That's not to say, who was and wasn't qualified, but the common qualities of their preferences for employees were obvious.

Kennedy led me to a conference room, where a pretty blonde woman with an intense gaze and a kind smile stood up from her chair to greet me.

"I'm Natela," she said. "I'm a senior copywriter here."

"Anthony," I said. "I'm just a guy."

She fake laughed for a second, then abruptly stopped.

We talked about my experience. She wanted to know what I'd written, why I write, how long I'd been doing it for. I had no idea if my answers were getting me any closer to being hired. But she went over the hiring manager's head to hire me, knowing that I wasn't technically qualified enough for the job.

She showed me around the office. There was a kitchen with fresh salmon, avocados, all types of fruits, meats, vegetables, spices, herbs and seemingly every healthy ingredient you could think of, including their own products. That was another thing they'd gotten into. BeachHead Creative actually started off in the adult film industry, then they launched a line of dick pills. They blew up from the dick pills and transitioned into more legitimate, but equally seedy businesses like the cosmetic industry. The whole thing was surreal. Before they operated out of the office building, they were all sharing rooms in some mansion. In hushed tones, the employees would talk about the mansion parties and early days when BeachHead Creative was somehow even less transparent. I'm not knocking them. They ran an empire in its own right. But we'll get to all of that later.

Anyway, you could cook up a meal whenever you'd like — as long as you got your work done. A yoga instructor would come in to teach once a week and a meditation instructor would lead mindful meditation every other week. They were building out a gym and a locker room on the first floor to have a crossfit instructor come in and train employees every day before work. Employees would bring their pets to the office. It was a millennial's wet dream.

My first official day at work, I met the writing team. Trevor, the head copywriter, had stringy long hair that he alternated between letting it hang down and wearing it up in a ponytail. He usually wore a plain white t-shirt, jeans and Chuck Taylor's. He had bags under his eyes and a patchy mustache and goatee and he was well-worn from his drug habits, but he also had a strange charisma, a sort of spastic energy he saved for the most critical bursts. Trevor was right there from the beginning when the company was still into dick pills.

There was Tom, Kennedy's boyfriend. He was quiet and worked in his own corner. I never read anything he wrote, but they talked about him like a god and they let him work from home every other week. He was apparently damn good. Shelly was another senior copywriter. She was kind, direct and skilled. There was Adam. He had that cool, bad uncle vibe and was funny. He had written scripts and had a few of them optioned for a good chunk of change on the side. Adam worked directly with Andrew, a junior copywriter, who I became good friends with. Andrew looked like he could be Adam's much younger brother or maybe nephew. They dressed the same almost every day as if they'd coordinated outfits and they lobbed and spiked jokes back and forth throughout the day.

John was a quiet, nervous guy, hired around the same time as me. He was too fragile to last long there. Michelle, a cute little caramel skinned beauty from Miami, was the only non-writer in the writing department. She was smart, highly resourceful and was essentially there to function as the left-brain of the team, keeping us organized, helping us to prioritize and just generally keeping the team on track. She had her own radio show she was working to build in her free time. Something about women's empowerment. There was Bill, and an old guy named Ted, who Natela made cry three or four times. And lastly, but least forgettably, there was Natela, who I'd be tethered to from then on. She was from Georgia — not my Georgia, but the European Georgia of the former Soviet Union. Natela had a degree in journalism from Columbia University — the best program in the country. She'd worked for Sports Illustrated as a writer before BeachHead Creative. She was a lovely person, a brutal boss, a vegan and she owned rabbits and parrots, which she liked more than people most of the time.

The founders relied on the writing department to create content, and to brainstorm new products. That was part of the job. BeachHead Creative had these massive email lists from the dick pill days. Lists of hundreds of thousands of people. Maybe a million. All of the other departments were built around the copywriting team. We wrote scripts for video sales letters, email drip campaigns, banners. You know, stuff like "5 Things Your Cosmetic Surgeon isn't Telling You," the kind of fear-based tactic the grandmas fall for. "Write for the lowest common denominator," Natela would say. "If the middle American gets it, everyone will."

BeachHead Creative had manufacturing facilities throughout the country, where they made nutrition powders for health shakes, supplements, creams for crepey skin (which are really just wrinkles from aging), and more recently, magnetic eyelashes, which they owned the patent for. They used Kennedy as a model for an magnetic eyelash ad they plastered on an electronic billboard in the middle of Times Square.

There was Dean, who did controls and advertising optimization. He made electronic music on the side and had background soundtracks on the Kardashians and other reality shows, which he received royalties for. Then, there was Ester. I don't really know what she did, but she had her own office. Ester was Iranian, but she'd grown up in Canada. She had green eyes, olive skin and she always wore heels and rolled her hips like a salsa dance as she walked. She did pole dancing in her free time and she was sweet-natured and loved to travel and try new things. I wanted to talk to her, but I had a hard time not putting her on a pedastal and simply thinking of her as a human being. I'd built her up as this goddess in my mind. So had half the office. You'd hear her heels clicking on the floor and then see every guy's head turn like a dog eying a treat.

I Ubered to work every day at 9 in the morning, usually arriving by ten. I'd make breakfast in the kitchen before work started at 11am. Each writer wrote content on behalf of an assigned brand or product, following the schedule of different campaigns. It was the first job I ever enjoyed. For a while, I was on fire about it. At first, the only stressful part was having to learn some basic HTML for our mass emails, but all in all it wasn't too bad. I listened to ancient Japanese music, while I wrote. I typed away at my keyboard from the start of the day until around eight at night. Natela was a perfectionist. A real one. She didn't make mistakes. I'd stay with her in the office an hour longer than anyone else to work and learn and to do things her way.

Around that time, I found our first coders on LinkedIn, so development had officially started on StudyHubb. We were one step closer to the app being a reality. Whenever I had a second to spare at my job, I was messaging back and forth with the coders to coordinate the specifics of our app. Life felt like it was falling into place. A new job, a new apartment, and soon, we'd have a small taste of real success. A man always needs something to be proud of. Trevor and Natela were impressed and full of praise and I worked like a dog to prove Natela right for hiring me. During the weeknights, I'd light candles and either stay up writing novels and songs till 2 or 3 in the morning, or Vera would come over.

R.J. kept sneaking over to the complex to use the sauna, and we started hanging out somewhat regularly. He was one of the few guys out in L.A. that I felt a genuine warmth towards. We'd go to the beach during the weekend and drink beers and throw the football around. I didn't have family out there and in a way R.J. became like an older brother to me. He moved into a swanky complex right down the street. It had a courtyard with a pool and hot tubs and grills for cooking out and there was always some type of party going on in the middle of it. To break in the new place, R.J. invited me, Skip, an elderly investor and film producer and Manny, an investment banker. He cooked us steaks with asparagus and portobello mushrooms. His cooking was heavenly. I'd forgotten what it like to have a home-cooked meal. But that was R.J. He was good to his friends and he made each of us feel like family.

"Meet my buddy Manny," he said. "Manny, this is our new cousin, Anthony. Anthony's got an app and he writes. Manny went to Penn. He's an Ivy League guy."

Manny pretended not to like R.J. mentioning his Wharton education.

"Don't do that, R.J.," Manny said. "That shit doesn't matter."

Manny had the thickest New York accent from growing up on Long Island and spending time on Wall Street in investment banking.

"They call this guy the Wolf of the Third Street Promenade," R.J. said, almost giggling.

"Stop it," Manny said. "They really don't," he directed to me. "There is no they."

To Manny's frustration, R.J. had told and retold the story to everyone they'd befriended. It turns out that Manny had gone viral on YouTube once upon a time. He was an investment banker and had bounced around companies as an interim CFO. He'd help them raise money and grow and then he'd overstay his welcome — but he'd tell you he was ready to move onto better things. In the infamous video, Manny was stumbling drunk in Santa Monica on the Third Street Promenade. Someone put a camera and a mic in front of his face.

Manny explained, slurring, that he was on the prowl for strippers and cocaine. The video was posted around the same time *The Wolf of Wall Street* came out. It was a viral hit overnight with Manny on the receiving end of an outpouring of internet shaming. He was fired from his job, and had to threaten to sue to get the video taken down. Obviously, it was still a bit of a sore subject. Manny was kind of a sweet guy when he was sober. The problem was, he was never sober.

R.J. would go into earnest diatribes against cocaine and drinking, then he'd disappear into a bathroom or any other room. He and Manny would come out sniffling, re-energized and ready to roam the night. R.J. indulged in everything he claimed to loathe. I think he was sincere in his own way. I think he really didn't like his own habits. In the time I knew him, I saw him try to go cold turkey on something every other week only to return to whatever he'd tried to kick with twice the hunger.

"We had a falling out a long time ago," said Manny.

"Six months ago, cousin," R.J. interjected.

"Anyway, a long time ago," said Manny. "We had a little brawl at Mariner's Village. The neighbors got involved."

"You ever see a guy named Ronan, fuck Ronan. Fucking douche," he added, interrupting himself. "Anyway, the whole thing got out of hand, but you know what, R.J. is like a brother to me, so if you're a friend of his, you're a friend of mine and that's that."

I didn't really know why he was telling me this. They bear hugged. Maybe it was the vodka or the cocaine. But I had the backstory of why he wasn't supposed to be at my apartment complex.

R.J. turned Shark Tank on the flatscreen after he served dinner. As we ate he went over to his tiny glass desk he'd set up against a wall. He drummed as he worked. He had dozens of fake social media profiles he alternated between. Some type of black hat marketing technique, he said. He'd stop drumming and press his ear up to the wall.

"The neighbors are Russian," he said. "They've been trying to hack into my stuff."

I wondered if Los Angeles attracts the crazy ones, if we become crazy living on the fringes of greatness or if it was some combination of the two. Maybe we're drawn there because we want to go mad. L.A. is a colony for the starry-eyed, the strange and the starving.

Chapter Six: Self-saboteur

During the mornings, I would make enough calls and send enough emails to maintain the quota to keep my job as a contractor at QuickRecruiter. Ricky tossed me stray links here and there to help me get the results needed to stay on board. Between the part-time work, the full-time job at BeachHead Creative, the app and trying to keep pace with my writing, I got to the point where kickball was the highlight of my week. Ricky and I loved our brief, but friendly interactions with John. He was down to earth despite having built a rapidly growing empire. He would ask how we were doing and actually want to know. And beneath that kind demeanor, there was a fierce competitor.

We kept our team ritual of playing drinking games at Busbee's afterwards. Ricky would flirt with Brooke, a feisty brunette on the sales team, who came every now and then. I'd go back and forth with Allison, the blonde that wanted to be Andrea. Ricky and I got a little bored and hungry and dipped out of the games prematurely to go eat by ourselves in the front part of the restaurant. We sat down at one of the tables and I pulled my notebook out of my bag to write and scribble ideas, while

Ricky and I talked about the kickball game and Ian and Brooke and Allison. I was buzzed, maybe a little drunk when our waitress came with a cup of water in each hand.

She had light brown hair pulled up in a ponytail. Her eyes were dark. Her skin was fair and she was comfortable in it.

"Hey, my name's Milena, and I'll be taking care of you today," she said. "Can I get you anything else to drink besides water?"

She looked down at my pad and sort of cocked her head. Milena smiled. She took our drink orders and came back with them a minute later.

"Are you a writer?" she asked.

"Sometimes," I said.

"I write, too. More screenplay stuff."

"Nice, so you're into film?"

"Yeah, I'm an actress, but I've got a better chance of really making a living at it if I understand the other side of things, and I write songs."

Milena had a sharpness to her. She could make it in this city because she wasn't naive or unfocused.

100

"We should get together sometime," she added.

I didn't know if she was interested in me, or truly in the idea of having a writing partner, but either way, it was nice not being the initiator.

"Yeah, I'd love that," I replied.

"Here's my number," she said, writing it on the check. "Text me."

I texted her a few days later and we made plans to see each other the next Saturday. I thought about her throughout the week at work until that day came. I kept thinking the way things started was a little too good to be true. It allowed me to play it cool and have things develop like a good story, layer upon layer. We met up at beach in Santa Monica. The sky was clear and sunny and the sand was hot, but a gentle breeze blew cooly through the air. She wore a bright pink hat, the kind a tourist would buy along the Venice Beach boardwalk. She was barefoot with bikini bottoms and a crop top and she was carrying a bag full of beers in one arm and a longboard in the other.

We hugged and I started to feel a little more certain that she was interested in other things besides writing. She didn't have a bottle opener and they weren't twist-offs.

"Do you have anything to open these with?" she asked.

I pointed to my chipped tooth.

"Used to use these bad boys."

"Seriously?"

"No, that was from a soccer ball."

Milena laughed.

"I like men with chipped teeth," she said. "Isn't perfection boring?"

What a pleasant thought. She looked at life's messiness as happy accidents. She allowed herself to feel deeply, but she was unbothered by the bumps along the way. That's a powerful combination for a creator.

"It really is," I replied. "I've got an idea. Be right back."

I cracked the beer bottles open on the corner of a concrete wall by the little grass park where the yogis and acrobats did their poses seaside. We drank in the sun and watched the people passing by, giving them dialogue on the spot. She told me about going from St. Louis to

Chicago for school before she traveled around Europe by train, living in hostels. The hours flew by as we baked under the California shine. We had already set another date for that night before the first one had ended.

We met back up a few hours later in the evening. I showed up a little early to the billiards place she suggested. There were dozens of pool tables and about thirty or so people shooting around. Milena walked in wearing skintight jeans and heels and her hair was curled. She was nothing short of breathtaking that night, but I had to play it somewhat cool. We hugged and she bought us a pitcher of beer. I tried to pay, but she insisted, which was refreshing. She went after what she wanted in life and didn't care for conventions.

Everyone was looking at her. I racked the pool balls and we started shooting and drinking. Several pool pros played on the surrounding tables. One of them started to try to give her pointers, subsequently showing her the book he'd written about winning a world billiards championship. She was gracious and thanked him for the tips before we got back to playing.

We ordered hot wings to share and drank the beer she'd gotten for us. I started off at ease with her. That spark was there, that energy,

I could feel it. But she had this idea of me and it gave me a part to act. I didn't have to be the neurotic, wild, strange, overanalyzing everything guy that night. She made me feel cool.

Ricky would always say, "Remember, you're the asset." We'd talk about that. The exchange of value. Some people say there's a pursuer and the pursued. Either way, she treated me like the asset. Milena wanted to know who I was, what I burned for — all the things I was used to digging for with other people. We held hands at the table and then we kissed. It was quixotic, intoxicating, electrifying and it happened because the moment was allowed to breathe. We stayed there playing pool and talking for hours. Then we got in her car and drive along PCH to Pacific Palisades and parked high up in one of the neighborhoods. We sat there in the car holding hands and talking and kissing some more with the city sparking below.

That's when I started to get weird in the same way I'd been with Susan; overthinking, oversharing, killing any sense of mystery and all attraction. I didn't think of anything as a forever deal, but I felt something, enough to be inspired to want to keep her around and see how things would unfold. But the Future is a fickle mistress and she doesn't like to be talked about. You can think about her, but she grows bored and uneasy and rebels against being told what to do. The Future likes to be treated as sacred, patiently coaxed and loved through steady and silent labor. She takes her time and can't be rushed.

In spite of that, Milena invited me over to her apartment the next night. She talked about screenwriting and acting and her dreams. We huddled up under a blanket on her couch and watched Amy Schumer in *Trainwreck*, which turned out to be fitting. I wasn't paying attention to the movie and I couldn't think straight. All the blood had left my head and gone somewhere else. We started kissing and touching and we moved to her bedroom. My confidence waned. I cared what she thought, so I became conscious of my own movements and myself. You'll be a horrible lover if you're thinking about yourself. I had this idea that if we had sex, she would like me. I was eager and nervous. She asked if I had a condom. There's a joke that getting a guy to wear a condom is like getting a little kid to put on a jacket — a lot of "I don't wanna's" and reluctant whimpering. I just didn't have one. She went into her bathroom and rummaged under her sink, but she came up empty-handed.

By then I was horny as hell and not thinking straight, and maybe that's why I committed the fatal mistake of telling her I liked her way early and in the wrong situation. And then, I remembered one of the things she'd said on the beach — her last boyfriend was twenty-three. In my mind, I was certain that somehow, out of the some tens of millions of people that live in Los Angeles, she'd dated Lizzy's Chaz. And I asked her that, while we were lying naked in her bed. From there it was one blunder after another until I'd talked my way out of the door and out of her life. She was sweet about it, but the little flame that was there was extinguished. It stung a little bit even though I'd only known her for a brief moment. It felt like I'd self-sabotaged and part of me didn't want to give myself a chance to fully move on with my life.

Later on in the week, I got to go to my first work party at BeachHead Creative. The bosses hired a dj, bartenders, blackjack dealers and a catering company and had the office decorated for a casino night, tricked out with Vegas-themed decorations. All of the employees showed up in tuxedos and dresses. I think that was also the first time I really recognized anxiety for what it is. I still wasn't ready to call it that, though. Instead, I simply started drinking from the bar. The drinks were sweet, so I had one after another after another. I hung out with Dean and Andrew most of the night and told Natela how much I loved working with her — which was true at that point. I didn't know how to play any of the card games, so I chatted with my coworkers. I'd lost count of how many drinks I had, but I went to the kitchen and called Vera to come to the party. She came just in time to lead my drunk ass to the stairwell, so I didn't pass out or do anything wildly embarrassing in front of my bosses.

We got back to my apartment and she helped me lay down. Vera wet a washcloth in my sink and put it on my forehead. She lit a candle and laid my head in her lap and scratched it. She deserved someone who could love her, but she settled for my desire instead.

I showed up to work the next day hungover, but my dignity was somewhat intact thanks to Vera. The job was still interesting because I was always learning something new. The world of copywriting was fresh. I read the ideas and writing of the great copywriters. David Ogilvy, Gary Halbert, and Gary Bencivenga — which I think was whose son came into speak to us about writing. The company invested in our department. My desire to be great at it was further stoked when I found out F. Scott Fitzgerald started off as a copywriter. He was my first writing idol, and still, the only author, who could garnish his stories with adverbs and make it work.

A few weeks later, Natela made Ted cry again. Her moods grew harsher. I admired her as a person and a writer, but it was like working with Meryl Streep in "The Devil Wears Prada" at times. The ancient Japanese music I'd listened to was unable to help me keep my zen going. Natela went on vacation to visit her home country Georgia and to make a brief stop in Croatia. I worked directly with Trevor while she was away. His edits were lighter, so I could spend more time actually writing and churning out content. I wrote about three to four thousand words a day during those few heavenly, stress-free weeks. Then she came back and my pace slowed again. The easiness of working with long-haired, wild Trevor made the contrast of well-meaning, kind-hearted, lovable, but ultimately brutal-to-work-with Natela increasingly unpleasant. A week later, they put Andrew and me next to each other. I was the youngest writer in the department. He was the second youngest and I believed he was more talented. To make up for that, my mission was to vastly outwork my friend. I'd hear his keys clicking away next to me and I'd type frantically to stay ahead, assuming that whatever he wrote was probably of better quality, so I had to climb through quantity.

Ricky noticed my energy was zapped by the time I got back to the apartment. He offered me a solution — Vyvanse, an ADD medication. I'd been diagnosed with ADD as a kid, but thankfully my mom didn't believe in medicating me. Instead, I learned to cope and eventually to thrive and find the gift in my differences. But I was starting to feel mortal and I needed an edge. I started taking Vyvanse before work. We affectionately nicknamed it Vitamin V, but really it's composition is almost identical to cocaine. And it worked. I became mentally superhuman. Everything was easier. I was hyper-focused. Before my train of thought would leave the station and I couldn't find the next stop. With Vitamin V, I could write faster, coordinate with the coders to move StudyHubb further along and work on the books and songwriting at night and then still have energy leftover to work out in the gym at one or two in the morning. And for a few weeks, there were no side effects. I wondered if this was what people without ADD felt like and how much potential was wasted just by taking the simple gift of average focus for granted. It was magical.

R.J. invited me over to swim and grill out that weekend. Manny sat in the hot tub smoking a cigar. A guy with slicked-back light brown hair and aviator sunglasses sat next to him. He was a couple years older than me, but he acted like money. He was cool, quick-witted and lovable with a hand-me-down arrogance I'd usually detest.

"That's Matthew," said R.J.

"Ay, nice to meet ya," he waved.

"He's Canadian," R.J. added.

"Nice to meet you, Matthew."

"Likewise," he said.

Matthew kept to himself initially. As I understood it later, he was this way because he wasn't fond of Manny. He called him "bad news."

We got into talking about what we do.

"He doesn't do shit," Manny interjected.

"Actually, pal, I'll have you know," he said. "I'm just on vacation."

Matthew stretched his words out, which had a way of getting people to listen up.

"So you're visiting?" I asked.

"I'm always visiting, my friend," he said. "I'm a citizen of the world."

"He lives in Mariner's Village," R.J. said as he handled grill master duties. "That's how we became buddies."

"He was a wild one," said Matthew. "R.J. has settled down a lot since I met him. Used to be trouble."

They talked like decades-long friends.

"How's that movie going, by the way?" Matthew asked. "The one about the serial killer Uber driver?"

"It's going," said R.J. "I'm talking to this couple about financing it, but I've also been brokering some deals for JetSmarter."

"Well, listen," said Matthew. "I know a guy who might be interested in taking a look at the script. I can pass it along if you want."

"Yes, cousin Matt," R.J. said smiling and waving his grilling spatula excitedly. "That's what I'm talking about."

"I'll set up a meeting," Matthew said.

Matthew talked about how he vacations during the summer months, but didn't drink for the rest of the year. He said he was in real estate. He'd graduated from UCLA. He bragged about how easy it was to make grades in the states compared to Canada, but he could do this because he had mastered the art of making everything sound like a fact in his casual way of speech. Matthew had a laissez-faire approach to life.

He would always say, "vivre et laisser vivre" — French for "live and let live." He was Canadian when it suited him. Jewish other times, but he was always himself.

Between R.J., Manny, Matthew and Ricky when he joined us every now and then, we had the beginnings of a tribe, our own little merry band of fucked up misfits. Matthew would call me and I'd call R.J. and R.J. would call Manny. We went out during the weekends like that all summer long. We'd go to James Beach and watch Manny try to talk to every college girl that looked even remotely single. But I admired his bravado. How one man's heart could bear that much rejection without shattering is beyond me. He was a honey badger. He'd get bit, shake off the venom and keep going after it. R.J. was shy around women, which was unlike his attitude in virtually every other situation. He was the complete opposite of Manny. He felt everything too deeply, so he swallowed his silent suffering, drank it down with vodka and let his demons out a little more and more as the nights went on. R.J. would be red in the face as we'd leave, partly from the alcohol and partly from some feud with his dad. "He killed my sister," he'd say. Manny would put his arm around his shoulder. "No, "You don't mean that." Manny would turn and repeat it to me — "He doesn't mean that." This was almost routine when R.J. would drink. It was like two different people were fighting for control of his body and his mind — the childlike, vibrant dreaming kid and something else that was born from a deep wound. Matthew was always entertained by all of this. At some point in the night, R.J. and Manny would split from us and Matthew and I would keep floating from bar to bar.

Matthew was charming enough that he could disarm anyone. He could hit on a girl he thought was by herself at the bar and then when the boyfriend or whoever she was with returned, he could get them both to like him enough for the boyfriend to buy the three of them another round of drinks. He told me he had a girlfriend back in Montreal. They'd take turns flying to see each other. I didn't ask questions or judge him because I'd been there before: uncertainty, boredom, selfishness, chronic dissatisfaction, insecurity or whatever other reason you want to prescribe it. Relationships are hard, being human is hard, but life has a way of sorting things out. Given enough time, energy, vibrations and frequencies attract more of the same. It's the mundane magic, the subtle power of our thoughts that fill the void with angels or demons in the flesh and make existence heavenly or hellish. I was stuck in limbo, getting glimpses of both sides. Maybe it was all just one big sneak peek to help me decide which direction to go.

At work, the vyvanse was becoming less effective. I needed to take more than I'd started with just to get the same sense of focus. I stopped sleeping for more than a couple hours a night. My insomnia came back and my mind ran at all hours of the day. They hired a Polish-American girl named Victoria, who fit the BeachHead Creative standard for attractiveness. She talked like one of the guys and had this surfer girl vibe and was just cool all-around. They also brought on two other hires around then — Angelique, a classically-beautiful blonde, who had been a contestant on *The Bachelor* and Ava, a Korean lawyer, who was a shade under thirty, but still shared the millennial mentality.

I started to handle larger campaigns and my banner copy was performing well on our A/B tests. It was noticed even if I couldn't see it or feel it. In the email campaigns, we'd write a series of value-driven emails that weren't directly promoting anything. Sometimes, it would be a recipe featuring foods high in Omega-3s, a message talking about the benefits of Omega-3s, comparing and contrasting them with krill oil and lastly, the sales emails. Limited time offers. Scarcity. We're running out. 100 left. 50 left. Lucky for you we're extending this limited time

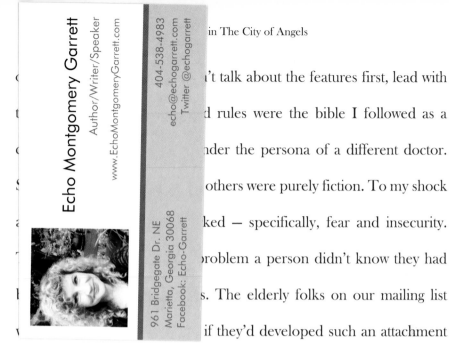

Echo Montgomery Garrett

Author/Writer/Speaker

www.EchoMontgomeryGarrett.com

404-538-4983
echo@echogarrett.com
Twitter @echogarrett

961 Bridgegate Dr. NE
Marietta, Georgia 30068
Facebook: Echo-Garrett

't talk about the features first, lead with d rules were the bible I followed as a nder the persona of a different doctor. others were purely fiction. To my shock ked — specifically, fear and insecurity. problem a person didn't know they had s. The elderly folks on our mailing list if they'd developed such an attachment to the persona that they'd invite the doctor to stay at their house, which did actually happen. Bill was invited to stay with an elderly woman in Paris.

BeachHead Creative was founded by three brothers and a friend. Tyler Thompson was their original writer and eccentric visionary. Jeff Thompson, the CEO, handled the business side of things. Tim Thompson ran the analytics and served as a bridge between the two. Lastly, Daniel Golden, the fourth founder, put up the money from owning gyms. Tyler, the youngest of the three brothers, had tattoo sleeves and usually wore ripped jeans and a v-neck. He was the least boss-looking of the group, but he lived the most boss life out of all of them, bungee jumping in Dubai, raging at Burning Man, flying his girlfriend to Catalina in a helicopter. I mistook him for an over-excited employee the first time I saw him. He was speaking at our weekly company meeting and hyping up all of the products. But the truth is, he was right. To produce the best results and the best writing, you have to find something to love about the subject. Tim was quiet and calm and worked at a standing desk near the writers. Jeff was charismatic and had the final say. Daniel had an office in the back. I'm not sure what he did, but I know the company didn't tolerate deadweight. He was funny when he spoke, but he mostly kept quiet and watched.

Jeff and Tim were actually fraternal twins, so they celebrated their birthday together. They rented out the Los Angeles zoo to throw a party for the employees. As soon as work was done, we packed inside the party buses they'd rented and we rode to the zoo. Back then, I didn't realize the magnitude of the people I was around. I was so focused on the next thing that I missed out on the chance to learn from people who had achieved incredible things. Tyler sat right in front of me on the cart that drove us through the zoo, but at the time, he was in another world. We pulled up to a section in the back that had been roped off for the party.

Cater-waiters walked around passing out hors d'oeuvres of exotic game and we ate all sorts of wild foods of dubious legality. Dean and I shifted our attention back and forth between casually eying Ester and watching the chimpanzees throw shit at each other. "She's a goddess," he'd say. "Completely," I'd reply. "The only thing," he said, "is she's into the jefe."

"Jeff?"

"No," he said. "Daniel."

I looked over at Daniel. He was in his forties, buff, unassuming. He wasn't flashy, but he was successful. There's a misconception that women want a man with money. That certainly doesn't hurt. But women want to feel safe. They want to see their partner has vision and burns for something. It's human to want to be inspired. I hadn't seen it before, but Dean was right. Ester eyed Daniel everywhere he went, looking for a way to get closer. We shrugged and turned back to the chimp enclosure. We were eating our food as the chimps resumed their shit-slinging. I thought to myself that we were witnessing a pretty good illustration for how we approach life. Here we were eating gourmet food. There they were slinging shit and they were probably having just as much fun. It's really all about perspective.

Chapter Seven: Better Angels

I started bringing a pad into the dry sauna at night after my late night workouts. I'd write songs with *The Eagles, Fleetwood Mac* and *The Rolling Stones* playing on a portable music device. I'd also bring a water bottle into it and refill it in the sink and stay in there for half an hour to an hour. Clearly, I'm made for hell. That infernal sauna also happens to be where I met a real life angel of a person. He had a sweet smile and was in his forties with a few stray grays on a head of thick black hair.

"Hey," he said. "I'm Cleve."

I introduced myself and we chatted intermittently as the heat of the sauna purified our bodies. He was a writer. He'd written for video games and movies, but now, he told me, he was working on a young adult science fiction series. Cleve glowed as he explained the premise. Before he made his living as a writer, Cleve was a cartoonist and an animator — something he considered himself to be a hack at. But he was damn good. We became fast friends, although we were opposites in our lifestyles. He made me believe that I had some redeemable quality as a human being that I just hadn't quite discovered for myself yet.

Cleve's dream was to make kids fall in love with science in the same way that *Harry Potter* made them fall in love with magic. He wanted them to see that science is the real world equivalent. On Sundays, he would teach children at his church. But most of all, he was always there for his friends. Some nights I'd go over to his place, which was decorated with illustrations, marine-themed antiques and items and paintings he'd done of famous Disney characters. He was from Orlando and had grown up going to Disney World. Cleve would turn on movie scores and classical music and we'd write together in silence.

Ricky and I still went to the Venice Beach basketball courts every now and again. We'd see acid Rob, who wouldn't recognize us, the crackheads arguing around the edges, the creepy ex-con, who always wanted to rebound for us and my new friend Bernardo. Bernardo was Brazilian with long, wavy brown-hair and pearly white teeth and he had a guru vibe about him like he'd figured it all out.

"My wife's a hypnotherapist," he said. "We run a subscription-based website."

"You make a living off that?"

"Oh, yeah," he said. "We work from home. Grace teaches courses online."

They'd achieved the real American Dream: living on their own time, doing something they loved. I hadn't known Bernardo for too long before he and his wife decided to move to Florida. They'd been renting a little house right on the Venice Canals. They invited me over for a going away party. Grace, his wife, was sweet and gentle and embodied her name perfectly. Their friends were artists, clients, musicians, actors and vagabonds. They wore big, wide hats, fedoras, string necklaces, crystals, summer dresses and other accessories. But there's always that one person at every party who wants to engage in deep conversation. That night it was Josh. He wore a wide-brimmed hat and a cotton robe and leather boots. He walked right up to me, cocked his head to one side then to the other without saying a word. He looked me up and down and then gazed into my eyes.

"You're an intense fellow," he said.

"I was thinking the same thing of you," I replied.

"You're a seeker of truth."

"What are you?"

"I'm a child of the Creator," he said, "and that's all I want to be."

"But what do you do?"

"Like the creator I create. And I roam the earth."

He paused again and looked me up and down.

"Do you believe in God?" he asked.

I couldn't explain to him that I was a Jesus-loving faithful agnostic. That would inevitably lead to him asking for an explanation. As these conversations go, best case, I'd simply agree with him and he'd be happy. His beliefs would sit cozy, snug and unchallenged. Worst case, I'd elaborate, we wouldn't align and he'd feel the need to defend something that doesn't require defending.

"Probably not the type of god you do if you're asking," I said.

"How so?"

Josh moved a foot closer and cocked his head again as if he was trying to find some new angle to peer into my soul. But religion is like politics. It centers around a common goal, but people blow things up and kill each other over how to achieve it. All religions focus on existence, mortality and ultimately purpose — the big question: why are we here?

"You believe that god is omniscient and omnipotent, right?"

"Certainly," he said.

"And he loves you like his own child?"

"Absolutely."

"Then he's omniscient and omnipotent, so he or it already knows who will go to heaven or hell before you even end up there?"

"That's correct."

"So he loves you, but if you're one of the bad seeds, he knew you were going to hell, where you'd suffer eternally and yet he still created you?"

"Yeah, well, I'm Jewish," said Josh. "I don't believe in hell."

"Okay, but you believe in the big guy in the sky?"

"Yeah, and it boils down to free will," he said. "God leaves the choice to you."

"Okay, I'm not questioning that free will exists. In fact, I'm not really questioning anything, but a benevolent creator wouldn't allow for free will. So to answer your question, I don't believe in a conscious god that loves you unconditionally under certain conditions that if you break, he has to disown you."

"So you're saying you're an unbeliever?"

"No, I'm saying that heaven, hell, angels, demons — all the language and sticking points of any religion exist on earth. Our reality is codified in metaphor and other terminology that we had to imagine as something more fantastical. We live in a world filled with mundane magic. Language and how we manipulate our thoughts, creates or alters that reality."

"What do you think happens when you die then? Do you think we just rot?"

I really hated to be the philosophical assholes in the corner of party. It almost made me miss watching monkeys throw shit at each other at the BeachHead Creative zoo party, yet there we were.

"People fear death because we have attachments to things here. It's more than an instinct to live. It's a desire to remain conscious. It's ego-driven. We want to still be ourselves. Why do you think people love a good ghost story?"

"Because they love to be scared," he said.

"No, because the idea of a ghost is consciousness or life after death. Becoming a tree or a cockroach doesn't excite most us because it's a pretty big downgrade."

"So if you don't believe in heaven or hell, then what do you believe in?"

"I do...it's just not a mystical place," I told him. "It exists here and now. So does immortality, but the soul are your vibes, your energy, your frequency. We change form just as ice becomes water and water becomes gas."

"But what determines right and wrong for you then?"

"Human beings have a general idea about it. Murder, rape, stealing, and lying are typically no-no's. Don't do anything that prevents someone from pursuing their own happiness."

"What if I don't see anything wrong with murder?" he asked.

"Then you're an idiot and you should probably be in prison."

"No, I'm saying without religion, what keeps people from doing whatever they want?"

"Does religion stop that from happening? Or do people twist noble wisdom and ancient truths to fit their paradigm and justify their desires and prejudices?"

"No, it gives people rules to follow."

"Like laws? The kind you get arrested for if you break?"

"Not all laws are just," he said.

"You're right. And not all interpretations of scripture or written word are valid."

He cocked his head the other way again. He smiled.

"God has a plan for you," he said.

"Thank you?"

"Don't thank me," he said. "Thank God."

Josh had just arrived back in Los Angeles after living in Israel for a year. I still don't know exactly what he did. He might have been a musician. That was the vibe he gave off after we got through the religion talks. Or he could have been a trust fund baby. Either way, he was kind and well-meaning.

Bernardo's friends were like that — deep, philosophical, open-minded free spirits. A brunette, slightly older than me, joined us. She told me it takes about three years to find your "tribe" in Los Angeles. Josh agreed. I stayed in touch with him for a little while as he globe-trotted. And I thought about the types of people Bernard brought together. They were quirky, eclectic and positive about life. I wanted to replicate his tribe.

I got back on Tinder. I had a love hate relationship with the platform. It was a good short-term salve for loneliness, but it's also part of the reason we treat people like they're disposable. Back when our grandparents wrote love letters, it took work to stay connected. Now it's too convenient to start over and for our bodies and minds to betray our souls. We say we don't care like indifference is a badge of honor.

I met a Thai-American girl named Mali after a long hiatus from the app. We talked for a few weeks before we actually hung out. She was in a similar position — in and out of something long-term and not really emotionally available. She was from San Francisco and had come down to L.A. for college.

Mali came over to my apartment after she'd been nannying all day. She was taller than I expected and had a fashionista sense of style. She was a joyful, happy person. Mali parked in the guest parking and got out with a bottle of wine in hand. We ended up swimming in the hot tub for a while. Then we went back to my apartment. We sat on my bed, backs against the wall. We uncorked the wine. I turned on music and we talked. We took turns drinking the Coppola wine straight from the bottle and we sang along with the music, louder and louder the drunker we got. She took pictures of us together on her phone. It was simple and uncomplicated and happy. She stayed over till five in the morning. I walked her out afterwards. But her car was gone. It had been towed, which was obviously not the best way to end a first date. She was pissed. We got ahold of the towing company and ubered over there and got her car out of the lot an hour or two later. Needless to say, it killed the mood.

The law of the universe seems to be that your luck or fortune, if you believe in that sort of thing, has to get much worse before it gets better. Ricky and I would say to each other that it was just the process of shedding bad karma. The StudyHubb coders ghosted on us after accepting a last payment. Between rent and development fees, I didn't really have the money to spend on food, so I ate mostly granola bars and whatever I could get from work without depleting the fridge or drawing too much attention. The sleepless nights, granola bar diet and Vitamin V uptick fueled my madness. And then Ava switched over from the legal department to the writing team. She said she was unhappy with her direct boss, so they gave her a swing at copywriting. In hindsight, Ava just didn't want to work at all. She struggled in our department and didn't like feedback.

I'd found StudyHubb a full-stack developer to continue what our first two had started. I wanted to make it successful and I had the idea that the job was interfering with my ability to take StudyHubb to the next level. Ava clashed heads with Trevor. By this point, I'd began writing from the couches in the meeting room instead of my desk, so I could communicate with our new developer without someone watching over my shoulder. I was still getting all my work done, but my head was in another place. Ava joined me on the couches to work and complain about Trevor. I liked Trevor at the time. I liked Natela even with the added stress of her work persona. But I started to think about quitting at this point. In fact, it became a fantasy of mine to just walk out the door, through the hills, right on down to Malibu and to simply not come back. A valid idea, but god, I was such a fucking millennial cliche. Ava was strongly encouraged to quit and I joined her after.

I spoke to Trevor and Natela alone. They wanted to know why I was quitting so suddenly. Truthfully, I just needed a chance to catch my breath. I asked if I could work from home one to two days a week as long as I got my assignments done. They ran it by Jeff, the CEO. No-go. They offered me a raise, but the money wasn't the problem. Natela apologized for how she'd been and she meant it, but the truth is, she wasn't the problem. I adored Natela even at her harshest. "We'll have you up to six figures in a year," Trevor told me. It sounded like an absurd offer, but Ava was privy to company revenue in legal. She claimed the owners made twenty million dollars a piece after taxes. "Writers don't make that type of money anywhere fresh out of college," Trevor said. Natela tried to get me to stay out of some almost sisterly instinct. She cared and I almost wished I'd seen that side of her sooner before it had gotten to that point. But I left anyway.

I still had my part-time work for QuickRecruiter and we could do that from the apartment, so I'd be alright for a second. Matthew called me the day before Fourth of July.

Chapter Eight: A Canadian, Two Strippers, A Con Artist, and an Unemployed Writer

"I met this super rich guy named Ellie," Matthew said. "He loves me like a son. Anyway, there's a party he can get us into tomorrow in the Colony of Malibu. You gotta understand, this is where DiCaprio and Hollywood really live. Are you in?"

The timing couldn't have been better. I'd just quit my job and was free to take that long held breath.

"Absolutely," I said.

"Great," he said. "We're meeting him at the Four Seasons Beverly Hills around noon. Come to my apartment and we'll take an Uber from there."

The next day we rode on over to the Four Seasons Beverly Hills. I posed with the Marilyn Monroe statue in the front of the hotel, pretending to give it a kiss. In my time in L.A. I didn't really spend much of it east of the 405, so it was nice feeling like a tourist.

Ellie was waiting for us by the bar in the lobby. "Ellie, this is my pal, Anthony," Matthew said. "It's great to meet you," Ellie said. He turned back to Matthew and hugged him as Matt winked at me. We sat down and Ellie ordered drinks for us.

"I met Matthew at the marina. He's like the son I never had. I tell him that," said Ellie. "Love this guy."

"I love you too, Ellie," Matthew said.

After a few drinks Ellie was telling us about his ex-wife and how she used to try to control him, but he said a lion can't be tamed. He told us when he was younger, he was handsome and had chutzpah and he was like a magnet. Ellie told us of his legend like the time he was in the airport and convinced a beautiful supermodel to change her flight and go with him to Miami. He bragged of having his way and ditching her there. He claimed she began stalking him.

"I'm good at manipulating women," he said.

"Ellie, Ellie," Matthew said. "You don't mean manipulating. That's not a good word. You mean flirting, seduction — anything else."

Ellie looked puzzled.

"No, manipulate. Convince them to do what you want to do," he said. "Anyway, when I was young like you guys, I could manipulate them. Make them melt in my hands."

"But now you're older and you've changed," Matthew said. "Right?"

Ellie grinned and patted his big belly and stroked his salt and pepper hair.

"I may have a belly and I may be an old bull," he said, "but I got chutzpah."

We went up to the rooftop pool.

"Are you sure about this guy?" I asked Matthew when Ellie left to hit on a Russian girl with big fake tits in a g-string bikini and a massive snake tattoo wrapped around her thigh.

Matthew glanced over with a hesitant expression.

"Yeah, Ellie's alright," he said. "He'll settle in. He's just showing off a little to prove he can hang with the young bucks, ay."

"Is he bothering you?" Matthew joked to the Russian woman.

"No, he's teddy bear," she said, grabbing Ellie's cheek.

"I can make you a star," Ellie told her.

"I don't need your money — though I'll take what you want to give me. I make plenty in my line of work."

"We gotta go soon," Matthew said. "Come on Ellie."

"I'll be back in a second," Ellie said.

"No, he won't," added Matthew.

She waved goodbye to the pot-bellied silver fox.

"Did you see that?" Ellie said as we got just out of earshot. "She wanted me so bad. As you get older you'll realize, the less interested they seem to be, the more interested they really are."

That didn't sound right at all. Matthew and I looked at each other. He left me with Ellie to go make a phone call. When Ellie found out I was from Georgia, he told me about how he goes to the Master's every year and explained how he golfed with Tiger Woods before.

"Tiger's putting is weak," he said. "I had a chance to play with him once and after he saw me putting, he asked for some tips. I fixed his short game. He practically owes his success to me."

Matthew strutted back over.

"My friends Angel and Skye will be here in about twenty minutes, then let's commence the night Ellie has mapped out for us."

"Are they beautiful?" Ellie asked.

"Ay, as beautiful as their names," Matthew replied.

We ordered drinks, clinked glasses to new friends and sat poolside waiting on the girls. They arrived about half an hour later. The five of us packed it into Ellie's Mercedes and he drove us towards

Malibu. He parked in a shopping center beneath Pepperdine College. We walked along the side of the road, cars whizzing by, the girls in their heels grabbing onto our arms. We arrived on foot in front of the mansions and beachfront pads of the Colony. There were trailers like you'd see on movie sets parked out by the street and security in front of certain residences to ensure that only the guests who were invited gained entry to their parties.

"This is it," Ellie said. "My friends John and Carolyn's place," he said to no one in particular.

He tried to walk right in, but was stopped by the hand of a security guard planted square on his chest.

"What's your name," asked security.

"Ellie," he said. "I'm a good friend of John and Carolyn."

"You're not on the list."

"Hey, hey," Ellie shouted past security. "Carolyn, it's me, Ellie."

A blonde woman in her early sixties wearing a pearl necklace and an all-white dress came from the courtyard.

"What are you doing here?" she asked.

"Carolyn, I've known you for years," he said. "And John and I are like brothers. Okay, okay, like long lost cousins."

"John and I got divorced last year," she said. "Go home, Ellie."

Ellie turned around red-faced.

"I thought we could party here," Matthew said.

"Eh, don't worry, my friend. The night is young and soon you'll be rubbing elbows with people you only imagined you'd see on the big screen. Come on. I know everybody."

We walked a few houses down and got denied again. Then, Ellie tried another.

"Watch this," he said. "Third time's a charm."

He leaned in close to the security at the third house and said something. The guard let us in. Ellie looked surprised.

"What did I tell you? Eh, eh," he directed to Matt.

We walked into the house. Everyone was beautiful and well-dressed, mostly in all-white. We provided a little contrast and were more eclectic in style. Two strippers, a Canadian, a con artist and a unemployed writer could be the start of a bad joke, but that was the makeup of our motley crew. Matthew disappeared among the guests with Angel and Skye went with me through to the back of the house facing the Pacific Ocean. Ellie just sort of vanished.

Skye and I grabbed plates and filled them with grilled octopus and seafood and other untraditional Fourth of July foods. We found two chairs to sit and eat and watch the sunset pink waves gently unfold like petals onto the shore. A few fireworks shot off from boats on the horizon and intermittently, someone would fireworks a few houses down. We'd settled into our seats just long enough for Skye to explain that she worked at the bar of a club, but wasn't a dancer. A moment later, a young blonde woman in her late twenties with a clipboard in her hand stormed up to us. "You need to leave," she demanded. I shamelessly scooped ceviche onto my plate and ate it as we were being hurried out.

Matthew and Angel had been kicked out just a few minutes before us, so the four of us were reunited at the curb. Ellie was missing. He tried to call Matthew a few times, but Matt rejected the calls because he was annoyed that Ellie turned out to be a bit of a fraud. We called an Uber to take us to Mariner's Village to watch the fireworks with Matthew's stripper friends. He turned off his phone after Ellie's dozenth call.

We got to the apartment complex just in time to catch the tail end of the fireworks in the marina. Hundreds of people gathered along the walkways of the apartments that looked out into the water. We watched the bombastic display spread like spiders across the night sky. And as we celebrated Fourth of July and people of all creeds, orientations and aspirations drank and danced and stood awestruck and illuminated, it occurred to me that Los Angeles is as quintessentially American as any place in the country. It's a city accused of not having culture, yet it's an amalgam of hopes, dreams and fears with its twinkling lights leading hopefuls from Nebraska and Missouri and New Jersey in pursuit of something that may or may not even exist — but the simple fact that they come and bring desires, desperation and madness is what gives the metropolis a pulse, a magic that courses along the 405, PCH and all its disparate and distinct neighborhoods.

I called my uncle Mark around then. I'd been thinking about him a lot, especially with the world playing tug-of-war with my soul. He was the angel on my shoulder. His leukemia was getting worse, but he was optimistic.

"How are you?"

"I'm good, Anthony," he said. "I might actually be out there soon. There's a place in San Diego and another in Arizona that have the medicine I need."

138

"That would be great," I told him. "I'd love to show you around."

"Yeah, I think Tijuana, Mexico is the best option for getting the treatment though."

"Really?"

"Yeah, we've been researching how to beat this," he said. "I'm gonna get through this. Have to for my boys."

I was sure he would.

"You're gonna make it and we'll be back on the boat at Lake Lanier and you'll be cancer-free."

"I believe it. God's got a plan," he said. "How are you doing?"

I wanted to make him proud. He had always believed in me and I wanted to tell him that I'd done something spectacular. But I still didn't have a clue what I was doing besides spilling my lifeblood onto pages nobody had seen. His words stuck with me — have a short, middle, and a long-term plan.

"Well, I worked as an advertising copywriter and an SEO specialist at QuickRecruiter. Still been working on the novel."

"I'm telling you, those children's books like Chase used to read, would sell. You could write one of those in a month. You've got the talent. Think about the return on investment of your time," he said. "You could work on your novel and still knock one of those out in the meantime."

I thanked him for the advice. His words always sunk in later and I trusted him. I told him how excited I was to see him again. I didn't believe my Uncle Mark was really a dying man. He was a fighter.

Ava and I stayed in touch after the BeachHead Creative era of our lives had ended. She'd ask for my advice about guys and dating even though I gave her fair warning that I was probably the worst person to ask, considering I was the guy who got a girl's car towed on a first date, lost another girl's car — also on a first date, managed to scare off Milena by acting like a neurotic spaz, and moved to the literal other side of the country from the girl I was in love with.

She brought me melons and other fruits from her family garden and tajin in exchange for shitty tips about life and dating. Ava, like Cleve, was one of the good ones. She helped me trademark our name and our logo for StudyHubb and we talked about dreams. She wanted to start her own business or find her soulmate or get into real estate with the money she'd made in law. Sometimes Ava would call me with some update about how she'd had a breakthrough about her future.

"My sister is never wrong," she said. "She told me I'd meet the man I'm going to marry in January of next year. Isn't that crazy?"

"That actually is crazy, Ava," I said.

I think Ava is worth mentioning because she was like an older sister to me. The universe sends you spiritual reinforcements when you need them the most.

Chapter Nine: The Starry-Eyed, The Strange, and The Starving

Around that time, my Uncle Billy rented an RV and drove across the county with his son Gareth and my Aunt Diana. Uncle Billy left Nashville to move to Los Angeles when he was twenty-years old. He didn't bring much more than his talent and a guitar. His goal was to get a record deal.

"I used to stay out till two, three in the morning writing songs at the diner, while all the drunk assholes and douchebags were filing in and out," he'd say. "I didn't have a drink till I was older and by then, I'd given up. But man, when you want it, you have to be willing to give your life to it."

After driving valet and playing small venue gigs to make ends meet, he sent demos to the big labels. After about a year, he got his shot. They loved his music and signed him to a deal worth half a million dollars. He was young, handsome, charming, could hit just about any note, and could write songs that told the kind of stories that could make people cry tears of joy and sorrow. He was contacted by the Church of

Scientology, invited to the Playboy mansion, and treated like a prince. Word gets around if you've got something going on in the City of Angels.

However, being young has its blessings and its curses. You're shiny and new and people are attracted to the glow of someone who sees the world through starry eyes and rose-colored lenses. On the other hand, you just don't know what you don't know. He spent money on lawyers and agents and things he didn't need and the label signed Sheryl Crow at the same time they discovered him. And as she caught fire, they put their marketing and resources into her. He was chewed up and spit out just as fast as he was chosen as their golden boy.

Few things are as bad as they seem. His life went on, as did his career. He was offered a position as a staff songwriter in Martina McBride's label, but he tried to lawyer up and spooked them off. He traveled around the world playing in houses and bars and small venues and continued putting out albums. That's how he met Aunt Diana — he was playing a gig across the pond. She was a flight attendant and came to one of his shows. She fell in love with the American musician and he fell in love with the sweet, young Brit with her posh London accent. He went back and forth between England and the states and they were on again, off again, but they stayed in each other's orbit. A few years later, he got Diana pregnant. It was a boy, my little cousin Gareth.

My uncle kept touring and driving Uber here and there. My aunt still works as a flight attendant and they got hitched in Las Vegas the past year. They raised Gareth in England. He was about ten years old when they came to see me. He has light blonde hair like his mom and they started him playing soccer young and every time they'd come to the states, he'd want to kick and I'd show him new moves. Naturally, he brought the ball right off the RV when we met up over at the Malibu RV Park. I picked him up and hugged him. I hugged Aunt Diana and Uncle Billy. They arrived during the night, frazzled, but relieved.

"We almost died," Gareth said. "This massive bolt of lightning struck right outside the camper."

"It's true," Aunt Diana confirmed. "Even your brave uncle was terrified," she teased.

"We were parked right by the Grand Canyon," Uncle Billy said. "The wind was shaking the RV, rain beating down, lightning everywhere. Man, shit got real."

"Language, Billy," said Aunt Diana.

"Oh, shit," he said. "It got real. But seriously, I haven't been that scared in my life."

They made macaroni and cheese and rotisserie chicken for dinner. Uncle Billy and I stayed out talking at one of the campground picnic tables and drinking beers after Gareth and Aunt Diana went to bed. We understood each other's chaos and didn't have to communicate exactly what it was. We were both more comfortable with darkness and a wink and flirting with the facts, but keeping the truth to ourselves.

The Pacific Ocean stretched out like a starless sky. It's an apt metaphor for your early twenties — you have everything in front of you, but you have no idea where you're going. My uncle got that because he'd committed to a life of uncertainty, for better or for worse. He was a charming, lovable gypsy.

"You like it out here?" he asked.

"I do," I told him. "I miss the family."

"And Isabella?"

"Yeah, a lot."

"She's a good girl. When you really love a woman and she loves you, don't let it go," he said. "These L.A. girls are cool and fun, but they'll eat your heart out."

"I kind of hoped that we could build something. That's what I've wanted. Someone, who wants to dream and grow together," I said.

"But is it really? I mean, I don't know. I don't have the answers. I've been in your spot," he said. "I remember the buzz and the energy of this city, how it fuels you. But there was also a girl in Nashville I left behind. We loved each other and it haunted me for many years. It's both."

"Like life tries to pull you in different directions," I added.

"Just don't do what I did," he said. "Don't try to solve it with drinking and women. That's what ruined my career."

We gazed off towards the sea. The moon was barely peeking out from behind a cloud and the waves wore its light like little sand dunes.

"Did you ever feel like you were losing your mind when you lived here?"

"Yeah," he said. "That was the best part."

I crashed with them in the RV that night and we woke up with the sun. My uncle was happier and more comfortable there than I'd ever seen him in a house or any place that didn't have wheels. Keeping a bag packed was the exact thing that made him want to stay.

Gareth got up and we kicked the soccer ball around, while my uncle went to do laundry. He carried a basket of clothes with him. After he'd been gone for a minute, Diana made Gareth eggs and bacon. I went to help Uncle K with laundry. He was chatting up a woman, who looked about thirty. He wasn't flirting with any intention other than to entertain himself and her.

Her name was Josie. And her mom and dad just so happened to be from England. Well, somehow or another, her family and ours wound up at the beach together. We played soccer and played in the waves and we shared beers, which was apparently not allowed. Two cops came up to tell us so. Thankfully, my uncle had his England I.D. on him and played ignorant of their rules. He even put on a cockney accent to make his case more convincing. Josie's mom and dad laughed and laughed about it after the cops were gone.

Our two families sort of became conjoined during that stint in Malibu. Josie and I started spending time together. She didn't expect too much of me and accepted a sliver of my heart. We'd go out dancing and play darts in the pub over in Santa Monica and when I needed a place to clear my head, her little duplex in Venice was all zenned out. She had a spiral staircase winding up to her bed and she always kept candles burning. We'd sit out back by the heat of her chiminea and smoke a joint.

Before my aunt and uncle and my cousin left Los Angeles, we ate at Malibu Seafood and hiked up Topanga Canyon. Having family I loved around, soothed that yearning for deeper connections, the subtle ache I tend to ignore. I showed them around my apartment complex, we said our goodbyes, and they were off again.

R.J. called me soon after. "Cousin, there's a fundraiser. Lots of movie people, lots of tech people. Movers and shakers," he said. "It's going down at the Beverly Hills Hotel. Let's have some fun with it. Invite cousin Pat and I'll bring Manny."

Matthew and I got all dressed up and went over to the hotel, where we met up with R.J. and Manny. The four of us were there an hour early and we began drinking.

"That's Sean," R.J. said, pointing to a long-haired Greek god-type fellow in a tight shirt and leather pants. "We're working on a film together. He's the star."

"Sean," he yelled.

"R.J.," he hollered back.

They hugged like long lost brothers.

"Sean, meet cousin Anthony, cousin Matthew, and Manny."

We shook hands. It turns out Sean was some kind of c-list action star on the rise. His breakout role was as some surfer whose girlfriend got kidnapped by the cartel and he set out to get her back and get vengeance.

When the fundraiser began R.J. ended up in the circles with the producers, the directors, and the actors, while the rest of us sort of mosied about. It was the first time I'd really witnessed R.J. in his element. He could get on well-enough here to appear credible in that industry. He knew how to speak their language.

I watched girls flock to Sean the actor throughout the event. He wasn't doing anything to draw their attention. In fact, he just seemed to know his value and carried himself that way. Because of that he was never desperate. Desperation is cyclical. The more desperate you act, the more desperate you become. Success is the same way. The more successful you seem, the more you'll attract it.

The once wildly popular comedic actor Pauly Shore came stumbling through the lobby drunk and alone. He was dirty and disheveled, but kind enough to take a picture with us when R.J. called him over.

"Pauly," R.J. shouted like he was talking to an old friend.

He waved and forced a smile and posed with our group. But he was the Ghost of Christmas future, a cautionary tale of how quickly stars can crash and burn. If you always play yourself, you forget how to simply be you.

Matthew got a suite at the hotel. After the event was over, Manny, R.J., Matthew, myself, and about a dozen of their friends went up and used the space as an impromptu after party venue. A photographer brought a bag of cocaine that everyone shared. He claimed to be the great grandson of the Edward Doheny, the oil tycoon. "My family built this city," he told me as he snorted cocaine off an eight inch steel blade. Matthew had decided to take a shower and was walking around the after party in a bathrobe like he owned the Playboy Empire.

A blonde woman and a guy, who could've been Lionel Messi's doppelganger, approached me. We talked for a while before it took a hard turn into conversing about polyamory. They were swingers. And polyamory is a bit like veganism, atheism, or drinking craft beers — if someone does it, they're going to tell you about it. It's a conversational compulsiveness, a need to recruit, or enlighten. She explained that they had an open marriage and her husband wanted to watch me get with his wife.

"I'll do it. I'll take one for the team," Manny interjected. "Pleasure to meet the both of you."

He shook their hands, and they quietly slinked away in apparent disgust.

"Ah, they're all talk," he said.

"Definitely," I replied.

I went over to the window and stared out at Sunset Boulevard. The city looked different from here. Somehow, it was this view of a city in limbo, straddling the holy and the damned, that appeared to be the edge of the world. More than Malibu or any of the coastal cities, which were the last places to see the sunsets in America. More so than the Pacific Ocean just beyond that even when it was a pitch black nothing during certain hours of the night. It was a hotel like this in this exact city that Belushi and so many others had gone just beyond that edge. I was more afraid that someday I wouldn't be able to see the edge anymore.

Chapter Ten: The Funeral

I was lying in bed with Josie when my second cousin Reed called. "Uncle Mark passed away," he said. We talked about him on the phone. Uncle Mark had been the closest thing Reed had to a father. I called my mom and dad. Then I cried like a baby when we got off the phone and Josie hugged me. Ricky came out of his room and I hugged him too.

I booked a plane ticket to come out for his funeral. I was a pallbearer and was asked to speak about him. I called Isabella and told her I'd be coming home. In a couple days, the whole family was back together. My older brother flew in from Montana to be there and to speak and serve as a pallbearer. Uncle Billy was there with Gareth and Diana. My Aunt Deedee was a widow now and my three younger cousins were fatherless. The funeral reception was open casket and when my youngest cousin saw his dad, he didn't believe it was him lying there or he refused to believe it. And when my grandma asked him why he said that, he pointed to his dimples and he told her, "he doesn't have these." His lifeless body didn't have dimples because he wasn't smiling anymore. And he was right. It wasn't him without the smile.

Hundreds of people came to Uncle Mark's funeral. Dozens of grown men were crying. My mom said it takes a great man to make other men mourn like that. She was right. His two oldest sons helped lower him into the ground after the service. I wondered how my aunt was even able to stand on her own two feet and not fling herself into the grave with him. She stayed strong for my cousins. She was the only person who could match Mark's toughness and bravery. My aunt wanted to be alone with my cousins to mourn. The family went their separate ways after the funeral, but I stayed in Atlanta for an extra week.

I saw Isabella my third or fourth day in town. She wore a floral dress and heels and rosy-red lipstick and all the old feelings returned tenfold on sight. What started out as coffee ended up us walking around in the park. The park turned into dinner and a movie and that magnetism that always drew us together, hadn't lost its pull. As fucked up as everything was, when we were together, face-to-face, all the confusion and the hurt melted away. And as much as she and I wanted to trivialize what we had because anything is easier than healing something that's been broken, what we had was it. The real deal. The stuff that makes the world go round and makes brave men out of cowards. The thing that gives this life meaning. Our love was born eons ago, spoken into being in a language that can't be heard by the ears, but is understood by the soul. It traveled through space and time and was born pure and only touched by stardust. Her name and everything about her was familiar like we'd met before in some other world. It was deja vu lived over and over again throughout each dimension of our multiverse.

But love and lust get tangled up like sheets and it's easy to confuse the two and mix the real stuff with the fool's gold. Or to not know you have the real thing because we're all cracked up Disney fairytales and you think it'll somehow complete everything. But it's not like that. Your pain, your hurts, your doubts, and insecurities are your responsibility. Don't expect someone else to heal you.

I was drawn in by her curves, by the way light played off her skin like it was showing me where to place my hands. Her lips always felt like warm summer rain and she was moody and wild and worth it because of those heaven-sent moments of ecstasy. And I wanted to pull her closer and closer and closer still, till our souls would be all mixed up and our fires would curl and we'd leave everything around us up in

155

smoke. Sheets turned to ashes. She was an addiction I didn't want to kick and the loveliest chaos I'd ever known.

Part of me wanted to stay. A big part of me. But I felt like California had more to teach me and I couldn't return to Georgia without anything to show for it. I couldn't come home having failed. I flew back to LAX a few days later.

R.J.'s belief that he was under cyber-attack from his Russian neighbors only intensified. He would pendulum from paranoia to a manic frenzy about the next big thing. He'd pop up from a desk mid-conversation and press his ear to the wall.

"When they're not fucking, they're hacking my shit," he said.

Matthew, Manny, R.J. and myself gathered at his apartment. He called an Uber and we packed in to go see an art show at one of the galleries in downtown Santa Monica.

"This guy's the real deal," R.J. said. "He was one of Tupac's photographers. He has street cred."

The gallery was full of pictures of Tupac, Eazy-E, Bone Thugs N Harmony and some other West Coast rappers I didn't recognize. I was looking for an African-American guy. But the photographer looked similar to R.J. Jet black hair, slicked back. A little shorter with a gold chain and a white shirt and jeans.

After he was done talking to a few admirers of his work, Matthew and I introduced ourselves. His hands were thick and stout, something I noticed when he made a sign with his fingers in the picture we took with him.

"I was always the only white guy around," he said. "They just got used to me. It's different when you have a camera. I was a chronicler, documenting history. Pac was cool. See that?"

He pointed to a picture of Tupac playing dice on the curb.

"That was Pac," he said. "A true man of the people. He was a real one, a gangster and a poet, and he didn't change with the fame."

"I love your work," Matthew said. "I'd like to buy this piece. What are you selling it for?"

"Three-thousand dollars."

"I'm good for that," he said. "I'm a huge hip-hop fan. I know YG and Young Thug."

"They're cool, man. Let's connect then and you let me know how you wanna do it. Most of these photos are limited prints."

They exchanged cards and R.J. was already itching to go to his next spot he'd set up for us. It was just a short walk down, not quite as far as The Bungalow, which I'd thought was as bougie as it got. 31 Ocean. The line was about a hundred people deep that night, and it seemed like there was a minimum attractiveness requirement to get in. Everyone looked like a model or an actress or an influencer of some kind or another. True fashionistas and studs.

"My girl Brandy is working tonight," said R.J. "Follow me, cousins."

I don't know why I ever doubted R.J. He got us past the line and his girl Brandy let us in without charge or being on the list. All the pretty girls flocked to the tables with the bottles and their sparklers to try to get drinks and whatever else they could charm their way into. I went round with Manny and Matthew assessing the scene. Manny would stray off for a short-lived attempt at one of the long-legged model types only to return. His pride was never wounded. I'll be damned if anyone ever embodied the old adage "You miss all the shots you don't take" better than Manny. R.J. was back to chatting up Brandy.

"Here's what we need to do," said Matthew. "We need to look like we're part of one of those groups with the bottles. That's how we'll catch us a couple bottle rats."

We couldn't find any seats at the tables, which were all purchased for the night. So we sat on the armrests of the couches and tried to blend in as best we could. In the process, we became the bottle rats, sneaking drinks when we were able. Everyone was so busy laughing and peacocking that I thought it might go unnoticed. But a guy in tight leather pants, the deepest v-neck I'd ever seen and a leather hat tapped a couple of his friends on the shoulders, pointing to us.

"You aren't with our group" he said. "We paid for this table. It's time for you to go."

"That's a great-looking v-neck," said Matthew. "Very Simon Cowell."

"Fuck off," replied v-neck guy.

We roamed around 31 Ocean a little buzzed, but not quite reckless enough to match wherever Manny and R.J. planned on taking the rest of the night. Probably to snort cocaine, find strippers, and howl at that great, big spotlight of a California moon.

"Let's go see Steph," said Matthew. "She's like my little sister."

We took an Uber back to the Marriott back in Marina Del Rey. The bar was still open. Matthew ordered us drinks and we sat outside by a fire that kept us warm. The valley stays warm, but the coast is chilled by the Pacific at night.

His friend Stephanie showed up a good fifteen minutes after we'd ordered our drinks. She was a pretty blonde with a quintessential L.A. style.

"God, I need a drink," she said. "Who's your friend?"

"Anthony," I answered. I went to shake her hand and she hugged me.

"Do I sense sadness in you, sis?" asked Matthew.

"He only calls me his sister because I won't fuck him," she said. "But yes, a little. The boyfriend is acting crazy again."

"Break up with him, Steph."

"You know it's not that simple," she said. "He's threatened to kill himself if I leave him."

"He's a grown man with a daughter. You don't need to take care of him."

"Are you single?" she asked me, changing the subject.

"Yes."

"Good," she said. "That's the smartest thing to be. Relationships aren't worth the drama. One second, you're fucking. The next, you're practically a step mom."

"Call your mom," Matthew insisted. "You know she can take care of this problem."

"I'm tired of her doing everything for me. I'm tired of everything really."

She gazed off.

"I just wanted someone to be obsessed with me," she said. "But damn, it's a lot of trouble. Being worshipped comes with a price."

"Your mom can fix all of it. Swallow your pride and call that woman. I know you, Stephanie. You need help. You're too kind. You give too much of yourself. He's a parasite."

"It's more complicated than that," she said.

"You love him."

"Yes," she said, "but I'm not in love with him."

We drank and we talked and she lit a cigarette. She was one of those people that always had to be altered. She could never be alone with herself. Untainted by a substance or a situation.

"I'm gonna do it," she said. I don't know if it was the drinks or us, but she called her mom right then and there.

"Mommy," she said. "I need help."

There was a pause.

"No, not rehab. I'm fine. It's Jon....yes...yes...I need him gone. I'm afraid....thank you...thank you...I love you, mommy."

She hung up the phone.

"What did she say?" Matthew asked.

"She's giving him a call," she said. "Thanks, Matt."

Ten minutes later her mom called back.

"What did you tell him?...and that was enough?...I love you...I will...it'll be a while...yes...goodnight, mommy."

"And? What's the news, ay?" said Matthew.

"She told Jon that she'd ruin his life and that she's make it her life's work to ensure he'd rot in jail if he ever came near me again."

Stephanie was relieved, but there was some part of her that seemed afraid of being alone, no matter how abusive or wrong the situation may have been. She needed the company.

We were walking distance from the Marriott back to the apartments. The three of us headed back. Her apartment was the closest, but she wasn't ready to see if he was gone yet. Stephanie said good night to Matthew. "Be safe," he told her.

I told her she could stay with me for the night until she knew her place was cleared out. "I need you to come with me to make sure it is," she said. It wasn't hard to convince me. It was stupid, half-gentlemanly, and potentially rewarding.

"You know I'm from Georgia too," she said. "Tybee Island."

"Really?"

"Yes, my father had a concrete empire that spanned all up and down the east coast and extended into Europe."

"Had?"

"He died when I was eleven."

"I'm so sorry."

"It's alright," she said. "Fuck it, ya know? That's life right?"

"Yeah, that's some of it."

"Ah, you're not jaded yet," she said. "Give it time."

She laughed as we took the elevator up to her apartment. Her complex was right by the yachts and you could see their sails as we rose up higher and higher.

"God," she said. "I'm not doing so well at this. I'm gonna make you want to kill yourself before I even get to fuck you."

I wondered if I'd misheard her. For all I knew in about a minute we'd open the door to her apartment and her psychopath, freshly-dumped boyfriend would be exploding in a frenzy. At least, that's about how bad he sounded and how high the stakes seemed to be.

But alas, she opened the door. No deranged psychopath. Just the nicest apartment I'd been in. There were clothes strewn about the hardwood floors and dishes on the marble countertops. She had her fireplace lit and candles burning and it was massive.

"What do you do?" I asked.

"You mean, how do I pay for all of this?"

"I wasn't..."

"It's okay," she said. "The concrete empire is alive and well. I'm an heiress. I've never had to work for anything and I won't ever have to lift a finger till the day I die."

She wasn't bragging as she said this. To want for everything and to want for nothing are separate curses, but each is a substantial burden.

Stephanie did a line of coke on a magazine.

"Want some?"

"I'm okay."

She shrugged.

"Oh, well," she said. "More for me."

I had forgotten why I'd even come. About the ex-boyfriend or any of the supposedly dire circumstances until someone knocked on the door.

"Can you get that?" she asked.

"Is it...him?"

"Go see," she said. "Grab a kitchen knife just in case."

"What?"

"Like in case you have to kill him," she said. "I mean, you probably won't, but like, just in case."

I looked through the peephole.

"It's some girl," I said to Stephanie.

"Phew," she replied. "That's my best friend Allison. She's been living with me. Let her in."

Allison was friendly and unsurprised to see a new man in their space. She was an art student, who waitressed at night and lived rent-free with Stephanie. Her main job was to tell Stephanie what she wanted to hear.

"I'm gonna order wine and food," said Stephanie. "What do you guys want?"

"I'm okay. Thank you though."

"Don't be shy," she said.

"I'll get ravioli," Allison said.

"I'm gonna order a steak for you," Stephanie said. "Every man loves their meat."

She ordered the food and wine on an app, then she called her dealer, who brought her xanax and weed. Comfort is an especially insidious kind of addiction like carbon monoxide poisoning. It'll kill you silently. .

The three of us smoked her weed and shared a few glasses of wine as they downloaded their days onto each other. Stephanie's phone buzzed about thirty separate times, but she seemed at ease blocking out the ex for the night. Eventually, Allison went to her room. Stephanie and I went to hers. There was passion on the surface. There was movement and frenzy, but her eyes were hollow. Her skin was warm, but beneath that, she was empty. After we finished she stared at me.

"Am I beautiful?" she asked.

"Of course," I replied.

"Do you want me?"

"I'm with you right now."

"But do you want me? Like to be with me?"

"You just broke up with your boyfriend. Don't you think that I'd be a rebound?"

"They never want to stay."

She got up stark naked and went to the bathroom to take her xanax. It zombified her. That's what she wanted. To not be there or anywhere. In the morning, her heart had hardened back up. Stephanie was reminded of the one thing an heiress couldn't buy and she resented it.

"Don't tell Matthew, okay?"

"Okay."

"He worries about me."

Nobody could save her, and I'm not sure she wanted to be saved.

Chapter Eleven: La Misma Luna

Ricky showed me a spot when we first got out there. A place he said had special energy. I used to run from Venice Beach all the way down to his sacred spot at night. It was the end of the jetty, where the sailboats would turn out from the marina into the sea. In the dark, dozens of sea lions barked and growled and grunted and rested on the rocks. The wind and sea lions' wailing provided the ambient noise when Ricky and I would meditate on the benches. I imagined his meditations consisted of sending the strength and courage he'd used to change his own life.

The Santa Monica Ferris Wheel shifted colors as it spun round and round like a great, big neon wheel stuck in the sand, trying to drive the only truly free part of the country away from the rest of it. In the other direction, airplanes flew in and out of LAX, shipping the new arrivals in as fast as they shipped them out. I imagined Isabella flying in on one of them to come see me. I knew she wouldn't, but it made me feel closer to her. Most of the time the haze and the light kept the stars well-covered up, so I pretended the planes were shooting stars instead.

That was my meditation. When the moon was visible I'd talk at it, not to it, not quite. I didn't believe in prayer. In fact, I thought my prayers were cursed because someone died whenever I prayed, so I'd just put my feelings out there into the wind.

In Spanish there's a phrase — la misma luna — which means, the same moon. It's something you can tell yourself, something to soothe your soul when it's full of longing. That's what I did. I thought about how she was back in Georgia living and breathing and dreaming under the same moon. And there's a magic about the moon, just the simple fact that it's one of the few things lovers can share with 2,000 miles in between them.

In the meantime, however, I got back on Tinder after deleting it for the millionth time. It's funny how we end up marketing ourselves like a product. Don't look too serious. Don't try too hard. Look candid. Write a funny bio, but don't make it too long or else they'll swipe past you without reading it. These days, everything is optimized. Put a picture of you and your friends to show you're not an unlovable leper, a picture of you and your mom or a puppy if you're really smart. And of course, show a little skin on the third or fourth picture, so you're not immediately written off as a douche, but you've got some edge. Enough to keep things interesting, at least.

I matched with a girl named Amber. She drove over to my apartment after her shift at The Rabbit Hole, an Alice in Wonderland-themed bar east of the 405. I had her park by the Marina after accidentally getting Grace's car towed. Her hair was dirty blonde with purple streaks in it and she wore a cosmic purple lipstick and she had ribbons in her hair and a psychedelic, ballerina-esque skirt on with stockings and heels and her skin was sun kissed. She was happy and easy-going and down for anything from the jump.

We walked to the backside of the complex along the sea-front units with their strung lights and music playing and people gathered for a casual kickback on their porches. All the units kept their doors and windows wide open, so their friends could pass in and out like the breeze. One group of pals drank and played video games. An older couple cooked dinner in the kitchen. Some of the older residents had been around since the seventies and had been renting ever since. They saw no reason to leave. Other residents would complain, but really we had everything we needed there.

"This is beautiful," she said. "How do you afford all of this?"

I liked how blunt she was. There was no game or play. She shot straight.

"I worked as an advertising copywriter. Right now I do SEO."

"What's SEO?"

"Basically, I get links put up for my company, so that way when people click them it drives traffic to the website."

I could have done what everyone out there does — I'm an actor, I'm in real estate, I trade crypto, I'm a dancer. To what degree never really matters just so long as there's an ounce of truth in the story.

"What do you do?"

"I waitress full-time, but I want to do something else. It's time for a change," she said. "I'm gonna go back to school and finish my psychology degree."

Most people make plans, some people have ideas and hopes, but few ever truly decide. Few understand the art of steadily chipping away like Sisyphus, forever pushing the rock uphill, forever enjoying the labor, learning to love the work as much as the idea of the thing, whatever the thing is. But she was going to do what she said. I could feel it. That's why she was beautiful and a force to be reckoned with — because she knew what she was capable of.

"My boss is also always hitting on us," she said. "And I won't sleep with him. Him and two of my coworkers were in some kind of weird three-way relationship. It's just unprofessional."

She certainly wasn't any kind of prude or strict with herself about anything, but Amber had her own set of morals. She lived in that gray area, where all my favorite people resided. The ones, who were honest about it, at least. The ones, who know themselves.

I learned she did kickboxing and she liked to go to music festivals and she wanted everything to be strong and intense and to make her heart pound like a drum. That's how it was that night. Pure heat, Ecstatic writhing. She was a desert flower. She did well in the heat. She thrived in it and could survive the harshest conditions. All the lovers who didn't give her love, who didn't give her a drop of rain. Still her petals were bright and flourishing. She wore her heartache like jewelry.

You always find out what things are in the light of day. She woke up the same person with the same feelings. The same ferocious lover. I started to like her as more than a quick flame. We traded energy back and forth and never really tired. Somehow, we'd ended up on the ground in a tangle of limbs.

"Do you date?" she asked.

"Of course," I said. "That's what this is."

"I mean like exclusively? One person?"

"Yeah, every now and then," I said. "When the right person comes along."

"But you have to be the right person when they do," she said.

I knew what she was getting at. Memories are a slow thing to thaw out and it takes patience to melt them away and form new ones. But she had a point.

"That's true."

She'd come over and we'd watch true crime documentaries, ones about famous people or conspiracy theories. But she knew that I wasn't ready for anything more than that. And by the time I started to like her, she'd given up. It was Jane all over again.

But the universe is full of hints about love and how we should treat it. Dusk, dawn, the moonrise, the rain, snow, the clouds, poppies, lavender, the fragrant honeysuckle perfuming the woods, the hibiscus closing itself up at night to save itself for the sun — each of these things serve a purpose. We're told you can only love a few things at a time, but the world was designed to teach us how to love everything in its

173

creation. Our hearts were designed to be cracked, chipped, bruised, stabbed, to fall in love, to be shattered, to grow right when it seems we can fathom its capacity, and above all else, to heal. We attract the people we encounter because our hearts require their energy and our souls have an unspoken way of calling them to us. The good and the bad ones.

R.J., Manny, Amber, Jane, Milena, Mali, Matthew, Cleve — they were dusk, dawn, moonrise, clouds, rain, snow, shadows, light, and whatever I needed for my path. Some people come into your life hard and fast like lightning, scarring the skies and burning what they touch to ash, so that nothing is the same as it was before them. Other people are rainstorms to bring you down, or to quench the thirst of your soul.

Keith Richards was a living chemistry experiment; heroin to bring him down, cocaine to lift him back up. I've always thought people can do just as well as any drug to regulate your mood. We're in a world of uppers and downers and numbers — they're all around us, living and breathing.

Chapter Twelve: Road Trippin'

Ricky flew back to Georgia to spend Christmas with his dad. He lent me his car to use while he was away. "You can take it anywhere," he said. "Just be careful with it and fill it back up when you're done."

I debated driving to see the Redwoods standing tall as twenty-story buildings, going to Death Valley or to see the explosion of neon lights in Vegas, the old glory of Palm Springs. I thought about seeing the Grand Canyon for the first time, or exploring San Diego. Finally, I made up my mind to go to Salvation Mountain. In Georgia, we had a an old guy name Howard Finster, who thought he'd been given a mission from God. He painted and built his own little whimsical place called Paradise Gardens. He was untrained like Leonard Knight, who built Salvation Mountain from the ground up. This style of art; outsider art, is honest and pure. If the guy in the sky exists, I imagine it's some of His favorite art. There's a rawness to it, like someone, who prays even though they doubt their prayers are even heard. My friend Robert always said he thinks those would be God's favorite prayers. Sometimes the value is in the doing. While Salvation Mountain was a celebration of faith for its creator, for me, places like that are worth visiting because someone took the time to search for meaning in their days.

I laid around for a while doing nothing. As busy as we try to seem, there's always more time. But that doesn't make for a good story. A cycle of jerking off, self-loathing, napping, and whatever else, is hardly inspirational. I got on the road around four in the afternoon. I passed Coachella Valley, where pretty people and fashionistas gather to show out for the Coachella Music Festival every year. Eventually, I reached desert. No gas stations. Spotty signal.

The sun was setting by the time I reached the Salton Sea, which has so much salt in the water that it petrifies the things that dare fall in it over time. Dead birds like little marble statues. Branches like skeletons. I almost pulled over to watch the sun disappear over the ghostly sea. I like cemeteries and mausoleums and deserts, where life and death dance. I like dried roses and ruins and dust and ashes and all the damned things, the things that were, but are no more. Things that fall apart.

But I kept driving. I passed Slab City, the true fringe of society, a scattered desert village made of junk. Rusted buses and vans and concrete chunks turned into homes. Its residents were completely silent. The last sliver of daylight was quickly fading as I pulled up to Salvation Mountain, painting the desert deep purple. And just as I did, a man with hair down past his shoulders and a grizzly beard with leathery skin and dust-coated jeans and shirt pulled the metal gate shut.

"We're closed," he said.

I could see it just one-hundred feet further. Salvation Mountain was whimsical, painted like an Easter egg.

"I can park here and walk to see it," I said. "I won't make any trouble."

"It's the holidays," he said. "People gotta get home to their families."

There was nobody around. Just us. I didn't know what people he was referring to. His other personalities? He seemed off. I'd heard about people going missing in deserts before. He wasn't a big guy, but he had crazy, take-it-farther-than-needed look in his eye. He had the physical characteristics of a tweaker mixed with the mentality of a Wild West lawdog. And what did he really have to lose? He reached his hand in his pocket. Maybe he was just itching his balls, or getting ready to pull out a cigarette. But it wasn't a stretch to imagine him pulling out a revolver or a knife. Perhaps because he imagined me to be just as much of a threat.

"No worries," I said. "I guess it's not going anywhere."

"That's right," he said. "We make sure of that."

"Have a Merry Christmas," I said.

"I'm a Buddhist," he replied.

"Go figure," I said. "Wouldn't have guessed."

I got back into the car and turned around and drove away. He watched intently until we were both out of each other's sight. I figured I'd seen what I came for anyway. I also considered not getting shot or stabbed by the twitchy guardian of Salvation Mountain a net positive. I rode through the desert in the dark, questioning my entire life. I wondered if maybe the simple fact was that I didn't really belong anywhere. When you get old, you long for youth. When you're young, you long for the certainty that comes with being old. The experience of being there and making it through it. I was always thinking of life in thirty, forty years, and calculating outcomes. Would I end up living in Slab City, spending Christmas alone, guarding some borderless patch of desert from the only company I'd get?

My mom had a travel writing conference near Palm Springs after New Year's. I picked her up from her hotel. We drove straight to Joshua Tree National Park.

"I've missed you so much," she said.

"I have too, mama," I said. "Whenever I felt like I was losing my mind, I could always talk to you."

"You still can, but I know what you mean," she said. "Same here, sweetie."

"When do you start to figure things out? When does life start to make sense?"

"It never really does," she said. "You just learn to love it for what it is."

We followed the navigation to Joshua Tree. It was obvious once we'd arrived — the Dr. Seuss-like trees cast their crooked shadows on the desert floor. And the mountains and hills of boulders rose from flat ground like the aftermath of a giant's game of jenga.

We parked the car in one of the campgrounds and walked around awestruck by the park. The landscape was surreal, everything was just a little off. It's the reason why the Eagles had come to shoot album shots and trip and George Lucas filmed parts of Star Wars there when he needed a location that looked like another planet.

In the suburbs and most other places, the days grow lighter and darker. In the desert, uninterrupted by houses, trees, or buildings, the landscape changes color entirely. It was a honeyed golden-orange as the sun set. Then, almost suddenly, it shifted. A blanket of blue put the day to bed. We drove past the silhouettes of the crooked joshua trees as the desert grew cold.

There's something sacred about Joshua Tree. I already have a love affair with the desert. It makes you sweat your demons out and then it cools at night like sheets after sex. Everything is dramatic out there: wide open spaces like a canvas for the sunlight and the moonlight to paint on — reds and oranges and browns like gentle eyes by day, purples and whites and blues like tears by night. The snakes and the scorpions and the heat can kill you the moment you become too enamored, yet so many things thrive in the desert — the cacti and the coyote with their separate tactics. And then there's the dust, turned into brick by time — a coincidental monument to the dead. Dust swirling all around with ancestral energy, whipping and wailing in the wind, imploring you to live.

"Your dad and I moved to New York right after college," my mom said. "Your dad had a modeling contract, and at the time, if you wanted to be a writer, a lot of the big magazines were in New York City. I was just a girl from Nashville and your dad was a boy from South Georgia. All we had was each other."

It started to rain a few hours into the drive. Harder than I'd ever seen it rain in L.A. Drivers there treat rain like we treat snow in the south. Traffic backed up, but it just gave us more time to talk.

"We didn't know anybody there, but I got a job working for Money Magazine and when your dad didn't have gigs, he cater-waitered and did odd jobs," she said. "It was never a sure thing. Nothing was, but that was what made it exciting. You were brave leaving the way you did. I miss you all the time, but it's what we do. It's in your blood."

I brought in her bags. I slept on the couch. My mom took my bed. I was proud to show her my place and she liked the stream of water flowing beneath the porch. The next day I took her to Venice Beach. The courts, the marijuana-scented breeze, the skateboarders gracefully grinding rails and gliding up around the skate park. I took her to see the Venice Pier, where the shore curves like a contented grin from horizon to horizon.

At night we walked the Venice Canals. The houses and the bridges were strung with Christmas lights, which reflected on the water. From there we walked to the rooftop bar at Hotel Erwin and ordered drinks. They had blankets, so my mom could stay warm as we looked at Dogtown and all around from a bird's eye view.

We took an Uber after our drinks to the top of the world. I had to show my mom the best view of my new home. I watched her look out over the whole city, curly red hair blowing in the late December air. She looked like a queen. I watched her taking in the views. My mom understood.

For her last day with me in L.A., we went to Duke's in Malibu and sat by the glass, facing the ocean. We ate as the waves misted the windows and the seagulls hopped from rock to rock below. Later in the day, I introduced her to Cleve. Two kind and kindred spirits. They mixed right away. He modeled the mom of his main character after her months later.

Back at the apartments, the complex was throwing an end of the year party in the clubhouse. Everyone was there. Cleve and all the other random characters I saw day to day. Dana, my friend, who was like a much older sister. And Kiyoko, a Japanese woman in her early forties

I'd had relations with. She was a graphic designer and a pole dancer. She smiled and waved coyly. My mom saw the look in her eye.

"You didn't...did you?" she asked.

"Yeah," I said.

Kiyoko breezed across the room to introduce herself to my mom — I wasn't sure she knew that it was in fact my mom at the moment, so I made that clear immediately to avoid any extra awkwardness.

"Kiyoko," I said. "It's good to see you. This is my mom. Mom this is Kiyoko."

Kiyoko looked relieved. My mom — not so much.

"You have very nice son," she said.

"Thank you," my mom replied.

"Okay, I go now," she said.

We didn't say another word about it

I took my mom to the airport in the morning and she flew back to Atlanta. Showing my mom around L.A. and Joshua Tree was the closest I'd ever felt to her. While the city is the virtual opposite of her personality — she is kind and gentle and sentimental — she was in her element there. Absorbed in all the gritty character details, the graffiti, the vibrations.

Chapter Thirteen: The Heathen Holy Land

Matthew called me a couple days after my mom left. He had a new adventure in mind, another round of mischief for us.

"Ay, there's a birthday party," he said. "A gathering of a few friends visiting from Montreal. We're meeting up at the Pink Taco for dinner in West Hollywood. Come, my friend."

It was always a good time with Matthew. We rode over together. The outside of the restaurant was a cotton candy pink and the famous Chateau Marmont with its Old Hollywood vibes loomed large on a hill in the background.

His Canadian friends were easy to identify even in the packed restaurant. They shouted ay's...ay, ay, ay...a chorus of ay's in the most Canadian way from their corner table up the stairs. We sat down. Matthew reconnected with his old friends, while I exchanged intros with them. We ordered margaritas and tacos.

"Lindsay Lohan comes around here quite a bit, you know?" said Matthew. "One of my friends picked her up here once."

"Isn't that like bragging about finding a penny?" said his friend Adam.

"Touché," said Matthew. "But a penny that was the main star in *Mean Girls*, the most iconic comedy of our generation."

Every stereotype about Canadian politeness turned out to be true from what I could see, and they were always smiling. Nobody complained. They just told jokes.

"I have an idea for a hit movie," said Matthew.

"What's it gonna be about, Matt?" asked Adam.

"Get this," Matthew said. "When people think of Canadians what do they think of?"

The other end of the table shouted their answers.

"Maple syrup...moose...hockey...snow...lumberjacks...that South Park episode."

"Precisely, my friends," he said. "They imagine us as lumberjacks riding moose guzzling maple syrup. But the U.S. underestimates their wiley neighbors to the North. What if we'd been biding our time for an invasion."

He slapped the table.

"Boom," he said. "The Canadian Dictator. Think about it. We're their worst fear. Socialized healthcare. In their minds, we are one step away from communism. Ay?"

"I like it," said Adam. "But it needs to be a comedy."

"We'll compromise," said Matthew. "The Canadian Dictator can be a dramedy."

The table toasted to Canada.

We finished our food and drinks and brought Adam along with us to continue the night elsewhere after the birthday dinner was all paid for. Adam was casual and confident like Matthew, but in a behind-the-scenes type of way. He owned several warehouses and did logistics.

As we walked up the street with no end in mind, we stumbled onto a little pub called the Den on Sunset. There was an outdoor part and an indoor section. The outdoor area was decorated with Christmas lights hanging over it and heat lamps to keep the guests warm on chilly nights like this. We walked down the entrance steps, which gave the pub a kind of cave-like feel as if it were a bit of a secret.

We went into the indoor bar and ordered beers. I sat down at a table with Adam. Meanwhile, Matthew found two women to chat up.

One was a pale-skinned brunette with a tramp stamp, the other one was a Latina with dirty blonde hair and a bad attitude.

"We dance down the street," I overheard the pale one say.

"Ay, my friends and I could show you a better time," said Matthew.

"Do your friends and you pay?" she countered.

"Absolutely," he said. "But first, let me buy you lovely ladies a drink. What would you like?"

He brought them their drinks. Adam got up and joined them in conversation.

I went out to the patio and sat down at one of the square wooden tables in the corner to drink my beer. I sat there watching couples paired up like mismatched socks, girls who dated their dealers, and your regular people who'd just come to have a drink. But the mixture of people felt almost intentional, fateful even. Then she walked in.

She had long, curly blonde hair and was wearing a white top with frills that draped over her chest and a black dress. My heart pounded with every high-heeled step she took. She and her girlfriend sat at the table next to me. I suddenly became aware of how my plaid sweater made me look like Mr. Rogers, but she managed to even distract me from my own insecurities.

"Hey," I said to her.

"Hey," she smiled.

She had a British accent with a hint of something else.

"I'm Anthony."

I sat down at their table.

"I'm Eva," she replied.

"Where are you from, Eva with the accent?"

"Manchester, England," she said. "My mum is Australian."

"What brings you here?"

"We're on a bit of a roadtrip across the states," she said. "We're going to the Grand Canyon next."

"Oh, my gosh," I said. "I'm so rude. I didn't even introduce myself to your friend."

Her friend smiled in amusement.

"I'm Katie, but please continue."

I turned back to Eva. I reached out to hold her hand and she took mine in hers. I wasn't really thinking about rejection, or how she'd react. I just did it because it felt right.

"I don't usually do this," she said. "But I'll let you."

"You're beautiful," I told her. "You should come to the beach with me tonight."

"Tonight? Right now?"

Matthew and Adam came swaggering over to me with the two dancers.

"The girls are ready to go," Matthew said. "I'm getting us a party room."

"Okay, one second," I said to Matt.

"Those your friends?" asked Eva.

Her friend had already scoped the place out and was ready to go as well. She tugged Eva in the other direction.

"Not the girls, but yes, the group," I said. "I'm about to have to go. Can I see you again?"

"We leave tomorrow," she frowned. "You have Snapchat?"

"Yeah."

We exchanged Snapchats and Whatsapp so we could message overseas. Her eyes pierced me like sapphire spears, killing my shame or sense of self. Matthew and Adam and I had roamed the heathen holy land cross-faded on tequila and the Next Thing; the next girl, the next spot, the next sensation. In the the shadow of the Chateau Marmont, where movies come to life and the truth is stranger than fiction, I found it — that rare certainty when your eyes and your heart and your soul all agree. When that happens, water doesn't matter, not food, not sleep. But she did. I'll never be ashamed of falling for a stranger. There's no pain, no hurt, no brokenness. You're not even really you. You're love and it's pure. I could smell her perfume still as we left with Matthew's new dancer friends. They were talking about money.

"You'll be able to pay both of us?" asked the latina.

"Ay, no problemo," said Matthew.

He walked with them on his sides. Adam and I hung back a few steps. We were along for the ride. I listened as Matthew told the girls he was a real estate mogul and a movie producer. Again, if anything had a hint of truth in it, it was fair game in L.A. The scale of truth is slanted differently there.

"Dave Chappelle is renting out a floor at the Chateau Marmont tonight," he said. "So I think we'll go somewhere else to avoid the crowd."

Matthew got our party a suite at the Mondrian Hotel. The room was fit for a king with a massive bed and a orange-tinted mirror that could be swiveled to face any direction in the suite.

"When you gonna pay us?" asked the Latina.

"Celia, he will," said the paler one with the tramp stamp. I think her name was was Layla. "I can recognize a gentleman when I see one."

"Does the Pope shit in the woods?" said Matthew.

The girls looked confused.

"Yes," added Matthew. "You'll be paid, but you don't get paid without services rendered, babe. That's just basic business."

Layla started to dance and undress. Celia frowned and reluctantly joined her. Adam and I drank wine and talked about business as we watched them give Pat a lap dance.

"Your friends gonna join or just watch?" asked Celia.

"We're good," we said. "Just talking." We turned the other direction, so we could keep talking and enjoying the views without being bothered for money.

"The show isn't free," said Celia as she danced.

"We're not looking," we said.

"Fuck this," she said. "Steph, I'm going."

"Calm down, Cece," said the other.

"I'll make more at the club. Cheap ass motherfuckers."

Celia grabbed her purse and her clothes and stormed out of the room half-naked.

Our little party turned into a sausage-fest after that. Adam and I left shortly after the stripper and Ubered back to Marina Del Rey. Matthew lamented later that he was left with a six-hundred dollar tab from the girls. But he boasted that he slept with the one with the tramp stamp and had impressed her enough with his prowess that he'd actually been the recipient of a discount.

Money was tight, so I got a job at an organic, health food restaurant called Lemonade. My boss J.K. was old school from Mississippi. He was great. My coworkers were easy to get along with. It was a fine job. After about two months of working there, I broke down. Out of nowhere. A customer order tuna. I think I got them sashimi instead of the ground kind. I had flashes of serving tuna for the next twenty years. I'd spent weeks telling myself how lucky I was to even have a job, but the reality was I'd gone from writing advertisements back to basically working in fast food. I walked out mid-order with my chef hat and apron on and never went back.

At that point, it occurred to me that I might never be stable enough to hold down a job for more than a year. How sustainable would that be? I started to feel like a marathon runner that cries and shits himself all at once as he crosses the finish line.

After Ricky came back from Georgia, I kept on exploring all around L.A. I could feel my time winding down. I visited Murphy's Ranch; the graffitied ruins of a former Nazi sympathizer compound, a lighthouse built into a cliffside in Laguna Beach, and Olvera Street; a street near downtown L.A. that resembled old Mexico with vendors selling handmade goods and authentic Mexican food — not that Tex-Mex crap that's been whitewashed with all the spices taken out.

We replaced our first set of coders with a new one, who worked on StudyHubb for a couple of months and bailed just the same as the first ones did. The truth is, when you feel like you're failing, you are. Your only real job is to be happy and to not hurt anyone in the process.

I started shaking again. I lived in one of the most desirable cities in the world and any stresses and troubles were self-created, but my mind was turning on me.

Ricky had been reading "The Power of Now" and listening to audiobooks on the way to work. He was still into mystical practices.

"Lay down, brother," he said.

I laid down on the living room carpet.

"Close your eyes."

Ricky lit sage and carried it around the apartment as it burned. Then he lit incense.

"Think of something you need more of in your life," he said. "Don't say it out loud yet. Hold it that thought."

He grabbed two metal balls with bells that rang inside of them. One had a painted moon and the other had a painted sun.

"Hold them out to your sides," he said. "Balance. The key is balance. Family, friends, passions, love, business. By themselves, these things are wonderful, but incomplete. Together, they equal a life of joy."

Ricky had also been reading about energy healings. He would move his hands over you without making contact, eyes closed, almost monk-like. And I don't necessarily believe in all that borderline miracle stuff, but over and over again I've felt it work and am temporarily convinced that these things are at play in our lives. Maybe our energy is as real of a substance as our flesh and blood.

Either way, Ricky's care extended my shelf-life out there. It could have been a symptom of the digital age, it could have been that we were living in the entertainment capital of the world, or it could have been some combination of the two, but I think you almost can't survive as a skeptic in a city like that. If you aren't looking for the magic and the meaning to offset the Instagram pop-up museum culture and the vanity of L.A. — that need to keep up appearances — your soul will age like a plump-lipped, botox-injected housewife marching along Melrose for her shopping fix.

Chapter Fourteen: The Prodigal Lover

Isabella and I started talking again after another one of our fallouts. I didn't know if she still thought about me or cared. But she did. I was on the verge of going back to Atlanta to see her. My birthday was coming up, so it was as good of an excuse as any to justify spending the money to visit home. My driver's license was set to expire in a few days.

I went to the Culver City DMV, but in California, it turns out you need multiple forms of identification. There's a fifty-fifty chance each day that I put my shirt on backwards or inside out. Needless to say, details elude me sometimes. It was March 5th, the day before my ID was set to expire. I went to the Hollywood DMV with two forms of ID, waited three hours in line, got to the counter. The worker looked at the forms.

"This one needs a signature from your landlord," he said.

"So you can't accept it?" I asked.

"Nope," he said. "It's not verified."

I weighed the pros and cons of burning down the DMV right then and there. I figured it would only be fitting to set that dull hell aflame, but in the end, the cons outweigh the pros. And the sadomasochistic workers could continue to do Satan's work uninterrupted.

The DMV would be closed the next day. Irrationally, I panicked, thinking I'd never be able to return home with an expired license or I'd have to retake the test and pay a fee, so I booked a ticket to fly to Atlanta that night. I packed some clothes and Ricky drove me to the airport.

"I'm gonna miss you, man," he said.

"I'm coming back, brother."

Some episodes of our lives don't end with a cliffhanger. In fact, it can be just the opposite — more of a whimper than a bang. I didn't know I was moving back home when I left. I didn't bring many of my things when I left and I didn't say goodbye to most of my friends and acquaintances because I didn't think it was goodbye. It's like they say, when you're a little kid, there was a last time you and your friends all got together and played outside, but you had no way of knowing it was the last time. Is that what it means when they also say ignorance is bliss?

Sometimes we make a choice we don't know we're making. That's what fate is, I think.

I was back at my house the next day. Then that night, all of my closest friends from growing up and my family came over to celebrate my birthday in the backyard. My Oklahoman next door neighbor, who had been like having a second mom, made jalapeno margaritas with tajin on the rims of the glass. We had homemade fajitas that we ate in the backyard on the porch by the granite-covered hill, a project my dad and I had completed right before I'd moved to L.A. It was like a dream where time freezes. My dad looked the same with his long hair and red bandana. He was over there telling a cowboy joke to my friends.

"So there's this guy," he said. "He was a huge cowboy enthusiast, so he decides to go visit a cowboy town in Montana. And he sees this guy walking in boots with spurs with a big ol' hat, and he says, 'Are you real life, genuine, bonafide cowboy? The guy says, 'Why, yes, I am.' 'What does a cowboy do? I've always wanted to see firsthand.' 'Well,' said the cowboy. 'You're in luck. I'm throwing a little cowboy shindig tonight.' 'Wow,' said the enthusiast. 'That sounds incredible. What do you do at a cowboy shindig?' 'There's gon' be some drinkin' and some dancin' and some fightin' and some fuckin' and some more fightin' and some more fuckin' said the cowboy. 'What do I wear for something like that?' 'Well,' said the cowboy. 'It ain't gon' much matter. It's just gon' be me and you."

All my friends were there, smiling, laughing and happy to be together. And Isabella came. Everything I thought I'd lost or was moving on, was still there as if it had all been waiting for the show to go on.

"I thought you guys broke up," my cousin Chase said loudly.

We pretended not to hear him.

"I thought you guys broke up," he repeated louder.

"Nah, buddy," I said. "We just took a little vacation."

My shaking was gone. All of my friends and family drank and ate on the porch. Isabella and I sat on a bench under the tree that was strung with lights spiraling up its trunk. She was breathtaking in her black and white dress and heels, and I was as happy as I get that night, thinking that the old and the new could exist together.

For once, it seemed everything was coming together. I was allowed to be myself. Intense and hands-on. We loved like we were starving, and I'd spend the night in her room, where we'd conceived our son, who was never really born all those years ago. We'd lay there in her turquoise-painted room with a candle burning, heartbeats coming back down to earth. The illusion was long-shattered — I was not any sort of gentleman, but she loved me anyway. And I loved her. She'd still ask me what it meant and I'd tell her love is what we make — not an accidental thing. It's a house of Polaroids and little snapshots distorted for better or worse by time. Her perfume was sacred to me like the oils they'd burn in the ancient temples and everything that mattered, seemed to be inside those four turquoise walls.

When you leave to go your old life behind in search of a new one, you learn what matters to you, what you value, who you want to be. You also learn the roots of your happiness, your hurts, your addictions. You understand the nuances of your needs. Why you crave sex, drugs, alcohol, television, sleep, whatever that thing is. The void is no longer just a void. It's a projection screen. When you're away from the familiar and your old context is taken away, you learn to chronicle the variables and the outcomes of the days.

I could no longer tell myself that my dissatisfaction stemmed from anyone or anything else, but myself. In fact, over and over again, Isabella tried to save me. My mom had. But before I'd gone away, I couldn't articulate anxiety or depression. I didn't recognize that it always lurks, but often strikes when you turn your back on it and pretend it isn't there entirely. And furthermore, that it's not your fault for struggling, but it's your responsibility to make something of it. Turn it into art, compassion, love, fuel. Just don't drown in it.

My fantasies changed. Instead of menage a trois and hedonistic daydreams, I wanted to go to church with Isabella, to move to Arizona with her and paint her in the desert and to volunteer together to play with kids. To have dogs. To have cookouts like we had by the lake years ago when we'd first met. To write her love poems on an old typewriter, while she watched the crime documentaries she loved.

But, as much as she wanted to forgive and forget the old wounds, she'd remember them and they'd reopen and she'd hate me all over again. Most of the things she said were at least somewhat true and certainly fair from her perspective, but I believed that I'd changed. I didn't think about other women and my wanderlust was replaced by a contentedness that had eluded me for most of my life. I was basically a racoon turned house pet, but I liked it. There's a quote that goes something like this: Find something you love and let it kill you. Well, it was working. The part of me that loved her was all that survived.

After a while, the insults starting adding up. I tried to put her first, to be compassionate, to understand that she said these things because she was hurt. The old patterns re-emerged after a few months of it. I didn't cheat anymore, but I questioned if it was worth fighting through it and my wandering eyes came back.

"You don't even love me," she'd say. "Why are you with me?"

"I do love you," I'd tell her. "There's no game. I wouldn't have come back if I didn't."

"You didn't come back for me," she'd say. "You came back because of StudyHubb or something else. God knows your reasons. I don't know if I even know who you really are."

Each time, there was little to say back. I kissed her and held her. I knew I loved her. I took her on dates and wanted to spend every second with her. Hell, I was obsessed with her to the point that it crushed me when we weren't getting along. What I didn't know how to tell her back in college was what I didn't know for myself — she was the center of my universe. I'd felt it in the shadows of my soul, but now she lived there and she became my home.

I just wanted to erase the bad. I had nothing, but love for her and I cherished all of our memories together. Our time was sacred to me and I felt like we could throw out the bad and keep the good for ourselves. But that was easy for me to say. In hindsight, my eagerness to move forward, while expecting her to be happy about it was like burning someone's house down and wondering why they aren't enjoying the beautiful fire in front of them. Broken trust isn't simply fixed by good intentions.

I decided to end things with Isabella. This time there was no ulterior motive. I didn't have any backup plans or an escape route. It wasn't even a matter of self-preservation anymore. I just believed she'd be happier without me and without the thought that I was ready to betray her looming in the background.

I read once that in studying monkeys, they'd observed that to maintain a healthy relationship in their groups, members had to have five or more positive interactions for every negative interaction. If only it was as simple as giving bananas or scratching each other's backs. For humans, it can go down the drain as easily as liking a butt picture on Instagram.

Chapter Fifteen: Atlanta

We finally found an app development firm we could afford. They were able to complete the beta and we launched StudyHubb that Spring. Our methods were questionable, but effective. Christian and I went to the campuses and posed as students to avoid being kicked off. We handed out sunglasses, wore Chewbacca and Yoda onesies, and talked to probably two thousand students in a week at one of the campuses, resulting in fifteen-hundred downloads.

"Bro, guess what?" asked one of the college kids. "Your app got me a date tonight."

At first, I thought it was a good thing. Bottom line is that people were connecting over our app. The aim after all was for it to be an academic social network, but the social part was important to us.

"That's great," I told him. "Hope it goes well."

Another kid I was pitching to told me he'd heard about our app on one of the campus buses.

"Yeah, this dude said y'all got a bunch of cute girls on the app," he said. "Like a hookup app. Tinder, but everyone goes here."

That's when we realized it could be a problem. Shortly after, we started hearing complaints from girls about how guys were being really creepy on the app. The negative reputation of StudyHubb got so bad at that campus, we had to leave because of rumors that our app was a prostitution service. I still don't know where that came from, but we promoted at schools in the city. Within a couple months, we were approaching almost 10,000 active users. Then the app started crashing. It wasn't built to be able to scale and it became virtually unusable.

Somehow or another, Eva, the curly-haired, blue-eyed British blonde I'd met that strange night in West Hollywood, and I started talking more seriously. As seriously as two strangers who met one time and live thousands of miles and a sea apart could, at least. We would video chat through Facebook and Whatsapp and we kept up with each other's lives. And she helped me when things fell apart with Isabella. We talked about dreams and meeting up again in California or England.

StudyHubb had ground to a screeching halt. Our app wasn't working, which prevented any chance of it going viral. We had no money coming in. My partner had quit his job to go full-time with me.

We were in the living room one night. I grabbed the whiteboard and a marker.

"What are we good at?" I asked Christian.

"Talking to people," he said.

"Yes, and that's part of marketing," I told him. "We start our own marketing company. That's how we stay full-time as entrepreneurs."

"Let's do it," he replied.

And right then and there, we created Blue Flame Creative, our brand new marketing business. We'd handle social media, events, content writing, and websites with the help of the third partner we'd bring on board.

We drove around town talking to business owners. Our first client was Red Martini, a bar and nightclub with an old speakeasy feel. They had hookah and sushi and it was frequented by A and B-list celebrities surprisingly often. Rappers, actors, the Atlanta sports teams. Their owner B.A. was a big, burly guy with tattoos, a bouncer's build and a serious face. His smile was at most a grin. But he was kind and easygoing. Still, you could tell, you wouldn't want to mess with him.

We got a massage chain as an account, a barbershop, a restaurant, and a couple startups. Soon, we had enough to build on and to survive. We weren't going to be rich from it at the rates we were going, but things were looking up. We did good with the nightclub, so B.A. set us up doing the same type of promotion for a seedy strip club that had been shut down ten years ago for prostitution. We met with the owner. His office smelled like incense and cheap perfume. He had a gruff New York accent and his legs were turning gray with cracked skin from cancer. He sat there in his worn down leather chair, bleary-eyed and broken, held together by his brutish will to live. To say he looked like Death would be insulting to the Reaper.

"The feds raided my house, my parents house, everything," he said. "They found nothing. Now we can be bigger and better than we were. I got clubs in Philly, New York, and Oregon. I own over fifty restaurants and clubs total. If you guys do good for me with this one, I can give you all of them to market for."

"We're the best at what we do," Christian declared.

"That's what B.A. tells me," he said. "The last guy who built the site tried to hold it hostage or something. He wouldn't give over the passwords. Guess what happened to the last guy?"

We both shrugged and let him tell us.

"The last guy is sleeping with the fishes," he said. "Courtesy of yours truly."

It probably wasn't true, but I wouldn't put it past him. He also told us about his adult film company. It seemed Luca had his hands in every seedy, underworld business. One of his managers came into his office with a large stripper who had a to-go box of mozzarella sticks in her arms.

"Who are these guys?"

"These are our new tech guys," Luca said.

"We aren't tech guys," said Christian. "We just do marketing."

"I don't even know what you're saying," said the manager.

The big stripper offered him some of her mozzarella sticks.

"I'm okay, hun," he said. "You need the fuel."

He changed his mind a few minutes later and proceeded to eat two thirds of her cheese sticks.

"These are so frigging good. You guys want any?" he said, offering us the rest of her food.

Luca's underworld success wasn't pretty or glamorous. And nothing could save him from his body's own attacks. He'd traded his soul to gain the world. We'd go in and take pictures of the girls for the social media account and their marketing materials. Some of them didn't want their faces in the pictures because they worked corporate jobs during the day. My feeling about that occupation was that it doesn't necessarily hurt anybody, they made good money doing it, and a couple of them seemed to genuinely enjoy it, but the vast majority of them just looked stuck, unhappy, and sure that it was the only talent they had. That's how it goes half the time: you're trapped as soon as you believe it. We'd be paid for our work, but I wondered what the true cost would be. The universe doesn't always send its invoice right away.

Some nights, I'd write poems and drink a beer at a table, while Christian took shots of the dancers. Any red-blooded man will admit that the views in that sort of environment get your blood pumping. It lent itself to good poetry. But afterwards, as Christian and I drove along I-75 back home, I felt the residual energy lingering on us like the dancer's perfumes and lotions wafting in the darkness. I thought about Ricky and what he said about being conscious of your energy.

"You know, it's exciting and fun in there, but that's not us," I said to Christian. "There's dark and light energy and we have to protect ours."

"Yeah, I know, brother," he said. "It's just a client and it's just business."

"Can you feel the darkness in there?" I asked Christian.

"Yeah," he said. "It's not us."

"Okay, good. We have to be careful not to absorb it."

Sometimes it takes going away to fully appreciate a place. I'd lived in Atlanta my whole life. When I was a kid, the Olympics came to town. The city pulled out all the stops. They built stadiums, new buildings, parks, and monuments. I still vividly remember the street fairs, the humid days and the buzz surrounding the city as we hosted the most celebrated display of athleticism and diplomacy in the world. It grew steadily after that, but it wasn't trying to impress anyone after the Olympics had gone away. That's until a few clever tax incentives and other factors made it a major filming destination. Atlanta became the Hollywood of the South, and by the time I came back, the city had a reason to build again. The skyline was dotted with cranes.

I used to think Atlanta didn't know what it wanted to become. The truth is, Atlanta has a strong identity, but it's subtle and paradoxical. It's a city blanketed in trees; a place that was once burned to the ground, yet is now built up to the sky; a place that was once the heart of the Confederacy, but is now the hip-hop capital of the world and a beacon of diversity; a city that's Southern and laidback in some ways and international and wildly ambitious in others.

I stayed talking to Eva, but I missed Isabella. I still believed I was doing her a favor keeping my distance. I was almost proud of it because it felt selfless. And I started to like myself in a way that I hadn't since I was a little kid, back in the days when you don't judge yourself because you're too busy picking clover and staring at bees. You're innocent and curious about the world.

I started hanging out with big Gino, an acquaintance I knew from college. He was six-five and played on the defensive line in college and he was jovial. Gino was a good entrepreneur. Hustle and ambition were two of the first things we bonded over. He was selling volkswagen bugs to a guy in Arizona for a profit of five-thousand dollars a piece. I had finally met my partner in crime for hitting the clubs. He liked dancing just as much as I did. Neither of us were particularly good, but we loved moving to the music. One night at The Warren City Club, our favorite spot, we got blistering drunk. I'm not an angry drunk. I'm a happy, invincible drunk and no idea is a bad idea. So I decided I'd jump off the balcony and land on the dumpster as we were leaving —

kind of like they do in the movies. But I was so drunk that instead of jumping, I rolled off the railing, missing the dumpster almost completely with the exception of my head smacking against it. It bounced off the concrete after and I landed on my side in dumpster juice. I had a travel assignment to write about a luxury resort in Los Cabos, Mexico two days later. There I was eating Zarandeado octopus, drinking mezcal and the forgotten spirits of Mexico and looking out on the Sea of Cortez with a cracked rib. I felt like the luckiest person in the world to have an opportunity like that in spite of myself.

After we'd saved up enough money, Christian and I started another app. This one was a typewriter app with all these vintage fonts. The letters had randomized boldness, so it mimicked the keystrokes of a real typewriter, varying in thickness based on how hard the typist clanked the keys. We charged a couple bucks per download and it turned out revenue-wise to be our first success in apps. Granted, it was modest, but we were thrilled after our heartache with StudyHubb.

We'd go down to the Beltline, which was this ambitious concrete walking and biking path that was built over the old train tracks. Bit by bit, the city of Atlanta was buying up new land and connecting sections of the path. The dream was to eventually create a circle around the city, so that you could get around it on foot or bike with ease. We'd set up shop along the path. Christian would grab the attention of passerby and I'd write them custom poems on the spot in exchange for downloading our app. I felt like the Jamaicans in Venice Beach hustling their mixtapes.

Gradually, I noticed other similarities to Venice Beach down in the Old Fourth Ward / Inman Park / Virginia Highlands area. The bridges and the walls were covered in graffiti and street art and these beautiful murals that told the mundane and the grandiose stories of the city. The best art is rebellion. There were depictions of Trump behind bars, stencils of him with a Hitler stache, another of him with a pig nose as an ode to Animal Farm. There was Black Lives Matter graffiti under the bridges and along the Krog Street Tunnel.

Much like the recurring cast of Venice Beach characters — the devil-horned speedo-wearing roller-blader, the melting-wax bodybuilder, the girl in the fedora, and acid Rob — I started seeing the same people again and again on the Beltline. The six-foot five photographer from Red Martini and the other nightclubs would bike around with friends. This pretty mom with her feisty cub, the two upstarts with their beverage business pushing their cart around, the fit

Brazilian girl with her soccer ball, the saxophonist who played Outkast. I knew bits and pieces of most of their stories. I made up others like one for the girl with the flower tattoo on her wrist with the long black hair that flowed like smoke and eyes that had seen everything. I decided she wanted to feel something new, just not as much as she liked being admired like the moon. Just hanging there high above your average folk. She'd speed by on her longboard. She liked dangerous things like snakes and scorpions and motorcycles and knives and anything that made her heart pound hard enough to remind her it was there still. She liked Motown and R&B and flamenco and pretty words. She believed in magic and would do whatever she wanted whenever she was in the mood.

There was a skate park right next to the graffiti-covered bridge like the Venice Beach skate park. I'd sit in the grass staring at the skyline of downtown Atlanta. At night, you could see the Bank of America building glowing like a torch with its yellow-orange pyramid and obelisk reaching for the heavens. It was a modern take on Art Deco, an Atlantan interpretation of the Empire State Building and the one structure that would make Atlanta natives think to themselves, this is a pretty city, isn't it?

I made it a habit to walk the Beltline even after Christian and I stopped promoting there. It became my new Venice Beach boardwalk or those long jogs up and down the beach from Marina Del Rey to Malibu. I fell back in love with the simple things like walking barefoot and shirtless in the humid Georgia heat during blackberry and lightning bug season. I became an observer again. I'd pass cookouts in Piedmont Park. Little kids running around, parents dancing and laughing, trap and hip-hop and funk booming on a speakerbox. We used to have church there in the park right on the edge of midtown when I was a kid. We were a gypsy family of artists and entertainers. No one had regular jobs. They were singers and dancers and painters and this place still held that energy for me.

Coming full circle made me see that life is a game of gaining and losing and gaining again. You long for love's rose, get pricked by the thorns, bleed a bit and the cut heals. You pretend not to see or know or feel half the things you do because then you'd have to deal with them. You carry these unspoken things like a bag of voodoo mojo, and that thing they call intuition is just patterns. You learn to read words that haven't even been written yet, and to hear things that haven't been said. You remember things that haven't happened because you were a memory before you were born and you'll be a memory again. And you know this because you're jaded. But between all that gaining and losing, you end up with you; the beautiful ruins of what burned down, the sum of the things that stayed.

Epilogue

We quit working with the strip club and I started to be gentle with myself again. When I was a kid, I had long hair and bloody arms and legs from an itch that wouldn't go away and I thought about death a lot and the meaning of life and I didn't act like the other kids. Eventually, I became more and more *normal.* But that's also how I lost some of the magic. The truth is, when you lose your strange, you start to die a little. "You" ceases to exist. The strange is what matters, the rest is just filler. So I started to also talk to myself differently and to replace the things I'd heard as a kid with new language. The only way you can be kind to the world is by being kind to yourself. I'd grown up wildly insecure, but you start to realize everyone is going through the same shit. If you look closer, you'll see the scar tissue of their soul. It's left by words and old memories. The Japanese have a philosophy about that called kintsugi. If an object is broken, they put the pieces back together with gold in the cracks to hold them in place. Instead of hiding the chips and the fractures, this highlights them and adds value. We aren't human without our imperfections. We're a living alchemy experiment, constantly being refined by pain, suffering, joy, love, sex, and death. The Buddhists would call it nirvana. Call it peace of mind, whatever you'd like, but we all have a gold soul in the making. Along the way, we're just learning to transmute our experiences and memories and the things we go through into something pure and meaningful.

Isabella called me one night after swearing she was done with me. She'd been out with her girlfriends. I Ubered to her and drove her car home at 4AM. It was a tequila-drinking night, a night for living and sighing and howling. A night for using each other's light to find the path to nirvana. My bones were full of kerosene. She was half-drunk and sparking. My words spilled out, my hands grasped for her in the darkness, and I lacked mystery. I just burned for her. Always burning. And she squinted up at me like a true child of the moon with her hair spread out like pressed flowers in a book, her skin painted by the light reaching its way through the trees and the windows. Her tequila-soaked kiss told me everything I needed to know.

I'd been clumsy with her love before; tumbling, slipping, falling, crashing into her. We collided with all of our being, every particle of us. Again and again. Our great, big, beautiful, clumsy, atomic love that froze shadows in place and made the earth shake like a four-post bed.

And when it was all over and everything was scorched from legs to lips, I remembered why we were put here. And why I stayed. In the end, all we have to offer each other is our scars, our recklessness, and our lives.

Most love stories end with guns drawn, daring each other to shoot first. That's also how most love stories begin: a glance, a shot fired, followed by a sudden piercing. The choice we make is death or sweet and mutual surrender; to rain down kisses or bullets. But this isn't a love story. Not in the traditional sense — no, a true love story wouldn't include strippers, drugs, unfaithfulness, addictions, romances, rejections and running away.

This is a story about being human, knowing one day, you'll turn to dust. But still, you smile and laugh and love fiercely even as you dance with Death. You take away its power by finding the things that start riots in your blood and bones. You burn bravely to ashes and pursue the light as relentlessly as a moth even as the darkness closes in around you.

Isabella and I went to see Disney's Aladdin at the historic Fox Theater. Built in the Roaring Twenties, it was originally planned as a part of a Shrine temple, giving it a Moorish design. I'd always told Isabella she looked like Princess Jasmine. She did, especially that night.

She had on a pink dress and her eyes were big and full of hope. The venue fit the Arabian night theme perfectly. I identified with Aladdin because he wrestled with love and wanting to be somebody and he was a douche sometimes. In real life, I don't know if Aladdin and Jasmine would have lasted. Sometimes, the feelings aren't enough. It takes rhythm, timing, and matching vibrations and frequencies. But I like the Disney way of ending a story, too.

R.J. had moved somewhere around Miami and was living off the rest of his dad's money. I learned the truth about his schizophrenia. He turned on his friends and stole from his dying dad, but I chose to remember Cousin R.J. for the steak dinners he'd cook us in his apartment and how he treated me better than family, apparently. Manny got jumped outside of a strip club a few months after I moved back. His skull was fractured.

Manny's heart was good and I liked him. He was just the guy who'd bring dynamite to a bonfire. Stephanie, the concrete empire heiress died of a drug overdose around that same time. Matthew kept doing his thing, harmlessly enjoying life. He had a Jesus-like mentality about befriending the sinner, but not for messianic reasons. Trevor, my old boss at BeachHead Creative, got fired for choking the yoga instructor, but he made the company a lot of money from his writing, so they kept paying him off the books under an alias. Natela and I kept in touch. We were better friends than coworkers. She was one of those hindsight angels you see fondly in the rearview mirror. Cleve finished his young adult novel and is well-underway with books two and three. Ricky found a way to thrive out there. He'd grown up in the middle of a greater madness. L.A. felt like order to him. He rose up to lead a team of fifteen SEO specialists, fell in love with a girl who loved him back just as hard, and he made the City of Angels his home.

When it's all said and done, it's a blessing and a curse that we go on living every day as if we'll never die; as if somehow *we* will be the ones to cheat Death, where our ancestors and their ancestors before them were overtaken. We have this unspoken hope, a hope not even articulated to ourselves, a whisper that maybe He'll have grown tired of his ancient work.

But the greater part of us knows this will not happen, so we look for the next best thing in love. Then, somewhere along the way, we realize it's the only thing, and we spend our whole lives trying to understand it. It's a force more powerful than gravity, but its physics are always changing, its rules being broken, and its logic destroyed. It's the one true religion, the one faith man needs. Without it, we haunt the world like a grandfather wandering from room to room, looking for something we won't find. With it, lovers can undress their souls and be as comfortable as if they were naked in their own home.

We try to find the perfect combination of words to capture it, to describe the feelings and the moments, what we love, why we love, how we love, and love itself. But this too is an impossible task since love wears so many guises, and if you overdose on any of its chemicals — the dopamine, the serotonin, the oxytocin — you may find yourself driven to insanity, paranoia, or hatred.

Because we know that hatred causes the withering of the soul, we know that love is the cause of its blooming. It's the mother of creation and as creation is infinite, there are infinite things to love. And certain types of love aren't meant to last, but to burn and to burn with such ferocity that in the end, you're left with charcoal and ashes — the tools to write in smoky letters or to draw in the honest shades of love and the real color of the heart of the universe. Not red, not fiery, not black or white, but gray like a graceful goodbye and a procession of souls passing through.

Longing turns us into ravenous angels
We are honey-coated, quantum lovers
particles entangled
She breathes like the flapping of butterfly wings
Her eyes, amber with memory
memorialize the moment
Her tender gaze gives birth to the mythic
suspending sands of the hourglass in the temple of philos
Yearning to be desecrated, we baptize one another in fire
We give each other silent hurricanes
and lucid dreams of frozen lightning
We climb the electric trellis to heaven
and find it is a bed of clouds for ourselves
cerulean and turquoise mist beneath our footfalls
the scent of creosote on the precipice of space
We can taste the stardust
from which we came, from which we will return
The ether beckons us home
to the void so we can find each other again and again
The silver of our aging heads is spun into gossamer
the unseen thread that strings she and I together
Stretched through time and space
our love turns life into an ellipsis
It is the prism of our existence, colored days, bathed in light
The silence cascades into a conversation that never ends
The echo fills the hollows
and another dream is conceived in the womb

Acknowledgements

I have to start by thanking one of my dearest friends Richard Fendler for going with me through the journey that inspired this novel. We grew up lifetimes in those couple years spent in the City of Angels and had a blast along the way, brother.

I would like to thank the brilliant poet and author Judith Kirkwood for your hand in editing the book. Your edits were much needed from a content perspective. I would also like to thank Fran Becker and my mom Echo Montgomery Garrett for your copy edits and affirmation that the rawness and vulnerability was integral to the story.

Travis Scarborough and Clint Crowe, thank you for being among my first readers and for providing immensely valuable feedback. Kristel Issa, thank you for helping me edit the final version, including those few tweaks to the ending.

Robert Hicks, thank you for giving my novel your stamp of approval and your honest feedback. You are easily one of the most skilled writers I've ever met, and an equally generous mentor.

Lastly, I would like to thank my Lucid House Publishing Co-founder Jawad Mazhir for helping me bring the poetry books I had written to market. Having them out there gave me the peace of mind that was necessary to write this novel.